SON OF THE AGE

LEE BEZOTTE

INSPARKET
— MEDIA —

Printed in the United States of America

Insparket Media
P.O. Box 1654
Moline, IL 61266

www.insparket.com

ISBN: 978-0-9976915-0-4
eISBN: 978-0-9976915-1-1

This book is dedicated to every fatherless son and every misunderstood daughter. To all abused, neglected, and bedraggled, abandoned but not forsaken.

CHAPTER ONE

COLD EARTH

SON WAS A SMALLER-THAN-AVERAGE TWELVE-YEAR-OLD boy. He had wild, windblown blonde hair and deep-blue eyes set above dry, chapped cheeks. His plain clothes were ill-fitting hand-me-downs that should have been retired many seasons ago. It was very early spring, and there were still patches of snow on the ground. Cold and blustery, the sky was a white-gray sheet that spread out overhead and never ended.

Though the soil was hard, it had to be prepared for planting season, and Son was doing his best to break it up with an old wooden hoe. He would often stop what he was doing to try to warm his hands. Unfortunately, he was doing a poor job of both warming his hands and preparing the ground. He wished very much that it was the end of the day so he could go inside and get relief from the cold, but he knew there were still hours to go.

While awkwardly breaking up the ground, Son heard his father call to him from the edge of the field. Obediently, he walked over and the man gestured for the boy to follow him to the back of the old wooden shed.

The wind stung Son's face as he stood there with

his father. He was a tall, rough-hewn man with rugged features and the unusual characteristic of having one brown and one gray eye. His hands were like rocks, strong and callused, since he had been using them for demanding labor most of his life. He didn't smile very often or show much emotion unless it was anger or disapproval. While Son's father talked to him, he rolled a cigarette and took a deep drag from it.

"I don't like you, Son," his father said angrily. "I don't like the way you are. Every time you're supposed to be working, I see you with your hands in your pockets. Did your mother teach you to be so lazy? Or did you get it from your witless friends back home?" He said many other words but they seemed to just echo in the distance as the phrase *"I don't like you"* sank deep into Son's heart.

Son had heard words like this many times before, but they still wounded him just the same. Since coming to live with his father two seasons ago, harsh criticism and long, angry speeches about his inadequacies were a regular occurrence. He wanted to defend himself. He wanted to tell his father that his hands were cold and he wasn't used to the conditions there. He wanted to say that he was trying, but the loss of his mother to mental illness, and the lack of any sort of stability, were weighing heavily on him and it was hard to focus on his work. But he knew better. He knew that to speak up would only stoke the fire that seemed to forever burn just beneath the surface in his father.

The man glared at him, saying nothing. This was even harder than the yelling because Son was uncomfortable with silence, and felt his father was waiting for a reply.

Though Son thought of many things he wanted to say, he dared not. He just looked back, feeling dizzy and sick, trying very hard to keep tears from escaping his eyes. He was unsuccessful, and a tear found its way down his cheek.

His father shouted, "Do you want something to cry about?! I'll give you something to cry about!" and he slapped the side of Son's head so hard that he tripped sideways, barely catching himself on the back of the shed.

Son wanted to cry out in pain. He wanted to run as fast as he could. He wanted to return to the land he was familiar with, but he couldn't. He found his footing again and stood there saying nothing.

"What are we going to do about this?" Son's father asked as he exhaled a cloud of smoke in the child's direction.

"I don't know," Son replied.

"What?!" his father asked loudly.

"I don't know," the boy said more clearly.

The weathered, middle-aged man let out a, "Hmmf," then took another drag from his cigarette and walked away.

Life was hard for Son. The land of Aun was harsh, cold, and gray. Even in spring and summer, clouds covered the sky, casting a drab hue over everything. Son had only seen a blue sky once before, on a trip to the Western Sea with his mother.

He missed his mother. She was beautiful and full of life. She had long, ginger hair, sparkling green eyes, and a warm smile that made Son feel like all was right with the world. It was just the two of them until he was ten and went to live on the farm, such a far distance from all that he knew.

They'd had a special relationship and, even though they'd had very little, they'd created moments together, singing made-up songs, taking long walks, and splurging on delicious fruit pies when they could get the money together or barter for the supplies.

But slowly, his mother began to slip. The weight of raising a child on her own, the abuse of her former husband, and the inability to adequately provide for the two of them caused her to retreat to safe places she had created in her mind. At first, she would just slip away for a few seconds. Son would notice a blank expression on her face and yell, "Mom!"

"I'm sorry, I must have drifted off for a minute," she'd reply, then smile and tell Son how much she loved him. Son always felt important to his mother, and was thankful for the life they had together.

In time, his mother's blank stares lasted longer and longer until, one day, he returned home from an errand to find her sitting at the table, lost in her own world, with food burning over the fire. Smoke from the charred dinner filled the room and Son yelled for her to help, but she just sat there, lost in her mind.

"Mom, come back! Mom, come back!!" Son yelled.

But she never did.

Son sat on the floor next to his mother's chair and sobbed, eventually pulling himself together to put out the fire and air out their home.

He draped a blanket over his mother's shoulders and sat across the table from her to watch and see if she'd come back. Eventually, he fell asleep.

The next morning, Son's uncle Kione came for a visit. As usual, he let himself in without knocking and saw Son and his mother sitting at the table. His uncle was not a nice man. He was large, overweight, bald, and abrasive. When he saw that his sister had lost her mind, he seemed more put out by the situation than sad for her condition.

Kione made arrangements for his sister to be institutionalized but he was not interested in keeping Son around, since it would mean another mouth to feed. He sent word to the boy's father and provided transportation for Son to travel the long distance to go live on the farm.

The days Son spent with his mother now seemed like a lifetime ago. Life was hard, the farm was bleak, and his father left him feeling insecure and unwanted.

It was evening, and there was still enough light in the sky for Son to wander outside, looking for some form of entertainment. He would rather be inside, where it was warmer, but his father was drinking, and the boy felt it best to stay away until the man was passed out for the night.

Since they had very little money, and what they had his father would spend on getting drunk, Son had no toys, no books, and no amusements. This, however, had the effect of expanding Son's creativity and resourcefulness. He would walk with his eyes peeled for anything along the ground that he could use to fashion into something he could play with. A stick and some discarded twine would become a bow and arrow, or a broken bridle and some stones might be fashioned into a sling for hunting. Once he even made a fully functioning miniature trebuchet.

He kept these things to himself, though, because his father never seemed to appreciate Son's creativity, and interactions with him only seemed to agitate the already irritable man.

When it became too dark and cold, Son went inside. His father was sound asleep and snoring loudly. Son sat on the edge of his bed to warm himself and watch the fire. As he watched, he carefully listened to his father's breathing. His father would snore, make a sound that resembled a man gasping for air, and stop breathing for a few seconds before going back to snoring. This process of snoring, gasping, stopping, and snoring repeated itself over and over until Son noticed that the periods of not breathing were getting longer.

Each time his father stopped breathing, Son would count, "One, two, three, four..." noting that he was able to count higher each time. This scared the boy. He wanted to wake his father to see if he was all right, but was afraid the man would get angry.

Son's imagination began to turn to dark places. What if his father died? Who would take care of him? Who would he go to for help since he didn't know anyone in the area? This went on for what seemed like forever; Son watching his father, listening, counting, fear, relief.

Then a strange feeling came over Son as he counted his father's breathlessness. It was a feeling of freedom. He thought, *If my father died, I could leave this horrible farm. I'm old enough to learn a trade and make it without him. I could go back home and be with my mother.*

Immediately, he hated himself for thinking such a thought. It was disloyal. It was selfish. How could he ever allow himself to feel good about the idea of losing his father? So he went back to worrying. He laid back on his bed and resumed listening and counting until the hypnotic dancing of the dying fire, and his own counting, lulled him into a restless sleep.

The next day was just like the others had been since he'd arrived on the farm. Son worked in the fields, tried his hardest to do a good job, stay warm, and avoid the attention of his father.

After supper, Son's father got up from the table and said, "I'm going out, and you're in charge," in a tone that took Son off guard. Son had never been told that he was in charge before. His father usually just told him that he was going off to the pub and left it at that.

Son said, "Okay," and mentally prepared himself for a long night alone at home.

Being home alone was nothing new to Son. He usually kept himself busy cleaning up after dinner, tending the fire, and amusing himself with the creations he'd devised while exploring the farm. He didn't like playing outside while his father was gone, though. Something about it made him feel unprotected. Even though his father was a harsh man, he believed that he would come to his rescue if he were truly in danger.

As the night was getting later and the fire was growing dim, Son began to worry about his father. The sky was black, the coyotes were howling, and the wind was beating against the little one-room dwelling.

Once again, Son's imagination began to go to dark

places, filling his mind with lurid images of injury and death. He speculated that maybe bandits had confronted his father on the way home, or possibly that he fell off of the high trail that goes around the falls; or perhaps he'd had too much to drink and was passed out in the street. Whatever the reason for his father's late return, Son found it difficult to relax on his bed and go to sleep. As it was, the boy rarely felt at peace. The unusually late return of his father caused his anxiety to tighten around him like a boa constrictor preparing for its next meal.

Eventually, the fatigue of early mornings and the demanding farm labor overtook his fear and Son fell asleep, restless as it was.

He awoke sometime in the middle of the night, hoping to hear his father's snoring from across the room, but it wasn't there. Only silence. The fire was now just a few glowing embers and the room was almost black. *Maybe he's just sleeping quietly,* Son thought as he groped his way over to his father's bed, only to find it empty.

Son began to tremble with concern as he made his way back to his bed. He thought, *Maybe it's earlier than it feels. Maybe he stayed at an inn. Maybe he'll be here when the day returns.* He did the best he could to comfort himself until he fell back asleep.

When the darkness had given just the slightest amount of ground to the light of a new day, Son woke with a start. He tried very hard to peer across the dark room to see if his father was there in bed. It was still too dark to tell, and Son was so very tired. Sleep pulled him back to his dreams for just a little while longer.

At cockcrow, Son was awake. The room was cold, but

he could now see everything. His father was not there. A heaviness came over Son that seemed to sap his strength.

He got up, got the fire going again, washed his face and hands, and made a piece of toast from some bread he found in the cupboard. He decided that it was best if he just kept going as if his father was there. After all, the man would be furious if he came home to find that the chores hadn't been done.

As Son headed out to the field with a hoe, he wondered what happened, wondered if he should go looking for his father, and wondered how long he could last on the farm without him.

Days and weeks passed as Son worked the farm. The labor seemed to come easier for the boy without the disapproving eye of his father on him. Once in a while he would see the man's tools, or catch the scent of articles he'd left laying around inside, and would miss him. There was a conflict inside of Son between missing his father and feeling relieved that he wasn't there to treat him poorly. From time to time, he would see someone walking in the distance and feel a mixture of hope and fear. Hope that maybe his father was returning, and fear of what he would do to him if he did come back.

When Son needed bread, he would walk to the nearby village and buy it using coins he found in a small jar in the back of the shed. No one ever asked him about his father. It was as if everyone assumed things were normal. This seemed strange to Son, but he was afraid to investigate because of a nagging fear that caused him to keep the whole matter to himself.

Day after day, Son rose early, worked the field, made dinner, and went to bed. It was always the same, day in and day out. Even though the work seemed lighter without his father there, the empty bed across the room reminded him that he was alone. The isolation added weight to his shoulders that increased with each passing day. His father was gone, he didn't have any friends, and he felt powerless to change his situation.

One day, while working the field, Son noticed three elder eagles rise from the tree line that was west of where he was standing. They would flap their wings only once or twice to reach a higher elevation, and then glide in a circle, riding the air currents until they wanted to go higher. He was mesmerized by the sight and found himself wishing he could rise above his lot in life with the effortlessness that the eagles displayed.

Why am I so earthbound? he thought to himself. *An eagle can soar above it all with but a thought, while I am held here like a prisoner.*

Then Son thought long and hard about his homeland. At least there were familiar shops and people there. He could even visit his mother if he wished. He deeply missed seeing her. He knew she wasn't well, but a broken mother was better than no mother at all. He thought about the jar of coins he'd found and wondered if it would be enough money to last him for the long journey home.

"I'm leaving," he said out loud to no one, and headed to the cottage to pack what little he had.

CHAPTER TWO
THE ROAD

THE NEXT MORNING, SON GATHERED what he had packed the afternoon before. In his bag he had a kitchen knife, the small jar of coins, some flint, a blanket, and a couple of other odds and ends that he thought he might need. The boy threw it over his shoulder and took one last look around the meager cottage before going out the door. Although he'd never liked living there, it was his home for two seasons, and a sense of nostalgia came over him. He had no fond memories and nothing that he would really miss, but he felt a certain sadness about leaving.

He looked at his father's bed and wondered if he'd ever return. He hoped that, if he did, he wouldn't panic because his son was gone. Even though the probabilities of his father ever returning were extremely low, Son left a note on the table. Since he didn't know how to read or write, he just drew a picture of himself walking along a dotted path, with his mother standing at the end of the trail. Then he signed it.

Stepping outside across the threshold felt like the most difficult step Son had ever taken. His legs felt heavier than usual, and the pack over his shoulder seemed more burdensome than he imagined it would be.

Walking across the farm and up to the road was like walking underwater. Each step was filled with fear and uncertainty as he moved further from the cottage and closer to a journey that was fraught with strangers, unfamiliar places, and possible dangers that the young boy was unprepared to face.

He didn't even know how to get to his homeland from here. He just knew that he had to travel west. *If I follow the direction of the setting sun, I'll eventually reach it*, he thought to himself, and he stepped out onto the long, winding road.

As Son walked down the road, he could see other farms in the distance. He noticed that many of them were in much better condition than his father's. As he went past their cottages, he could smell bread baking, see families doing chores together, and hear the laughter of children playing. It brought a smile to his face to think that maybe the world wasn't as horrible a place as he believed it to be. That even in a land where the sky was always gloomy, there was warmth to be found, if one just knew where to look.

He found a thin tree branch on the side of the road about as long as he was and decided to use it as a walking stick. Eventually he found his stride, walking at just the right pace. The triple step of his stick, left foot, and right foot created a rhythm that distracted his mind as he walked. *Rum pum pum. Rum pum pum.* The cadence somehow comforted Son and, for the first time in his life, he realized just how much he enjoyed walking.

For hours he continued at a sustainable pace, with his mind occasionally taking him to weigh the probabilities of his father's return. If he were to see his father again, what would he say? What if his father was dead? What if, what if, what if? He shook himself from the pondering of uncertainties and focused his attention back onto the rhythm of his steps.

Eventually the road took him up a long, high hill. When Son reached the top, he noticed that he was winded. He paused to catch his breath and look around. From this place, he could see a great distance in every direction. There was a very large body of water some ways off to the south that he had never seen before. There were no roads or trails leading to it from where he was, but he wondered what it would be like to sail across it. To the north, he noticed how the trees seemed to grow taller and change from leaf-bearing trees to cone-bearing trees. He had heard rumors about the people from the north and their violent tribal feudalism. He was glad he had never met anyone from there and was relieved that they kept to themselves. When he looked back to the east, he realized that he had walked so far he could no longer see his father's farm, even from this height. For the first time since he'd left, he felt the insecurity that came from traveling alone with only what he could carry over his shoulder.

Son turned his attention to the west, the direction this road was headed, and the destination he hoped to reach safely. He started to feel the first hints of hunger and wondered how he would feed himself. He wondered if this really was a good idea and hoped he had made the right decision. "Keep moving forward," he told himself. "Keep moving forward."

As the day passed and the road grew long, Son realized he was going to have to camp for the night. Since the stars and moon were covered by clouds, it would be too dark to keep traveling, too easy to stumble off the road.

From where he stood, he could see a village in the distance. He knew that the closer he came to the village, the greater the chance there was for him to be discovered trespassing and camping on someone's property. He looked for some high foliage, a stone's throw off the road, that he could hide behind and build a small fire.

By the time he found his way behind the foliage, the sky was a dark gray and Son struggled to see well enough to gather some sticks to make a fire. He piled the sticks behind the tall shrubbery and found small bits of dead grass and leaves that he could use for tinder. He then took flint and a kitchen knife out of his bag and began sending sparks onto the leaves and grass. It took longer than usual for the dead grass to catch fire; Son had to reposition himself continually to create a barrier from the wind. He felt panic setting in as his surroundings grew darker and darker; finally a spark caught the tinder and enough of a flame sprang up for Son to use. He immediately grabbed the burning grass, blew on it to stoke the flame, and placed it carefully at the bottom of his stick pile. It wasn't long before he had a small fire and a feeling of relief that he would have some warmth and light during the night.

Since he had no food, Son decided to just lay down and try to get some sleep. He could buy some rations in the village the next morning. He pulled a small blanket from his pack, but had no pillow or bedroll to lay on. He laid between the foliage and the fire. He figured that at least no one would be able to sneak up on him this way.

Since the blanket was only long enough to cover Son from his shoulders to his knees, he had to curl up considerably and get as close to the fire as possible, without sparks catching the bedding on fire. He shivered and shook, wishing he would have taken his father's blanket instead. Even though it reeked of beer and smoke, it was longer and heavier, and would have done a much better job of keeping him warm.

As Son lay there trying to sleep, he could hear howling in the distance as the night creatures began to stir. He reached over and added a few more sticks to the fire. He knew that the fire was the key to keeping dangerous animals away. As long as he had a fire, he'd be okay. Keeping his imagination under control was difficult. Was the scurrying he'd just heard a few feet away or at a great distance? Are there poisonous spiders in the foliage? Would he be able to break camp in the morning before anyone saw him?

Throughout the night, Son would wake up from the aching he experienced from laying on the hard ground. Whatever side he happened to be laying on would throb with pain until he turned over. He hated turning away from the fire because he was afraid it would go out while it was still dark. Eventually, when he was finally in a sound sleep, a flying insect, drawn by the fire, would buzz near his ear. He would wake up, try to kill the insect by slapping himself on the ear, and go back to sleep until the insect came buzzing back a few seconds later. This frustrating cycle went on until the sky turned from black to gray and Son could see his surroundings once again.

It was a horrible night of sleep, but Son survived it. Sore, tired, and hungry, he smothered the remains of the fire, put his things in his pack, grabbed his walking stick, and headed back to the road.

Though the village was not far off, it felt much further because of Son's fatigue. He was tired, hungry, and cold as he started walking down the road. The gray sky was giving more light now at least, and Son was relieved to be some distance from the campsite.

It was mid-morning by the time he reached the village. The walk had helped to loosen his muscles and he was feeling better, albeit hungry. As he walked through the village gate, he noticed mostly older people. They were gathered in front of the inn, sitting in front of their cottages, and coming in and out of the street market as they went about their daily lives.

As he made his way through the village, Son realized that most of the people were talking about him. He didn't need to clearly hear what they were saying since their looks and sniggers were enough for him to figure it out. He decided that he would just pick up a few necessities from the street market and be on his way as quickly as possible.

Upon entering the market, Son's mouth began to water from the smells of baked bread, roasted vegetables, and grilled meat. The narrow street was filled with vendors on both sides, and the path to walk between them was barely wide enough for two people to walk side by side. As he made his way down the street, he began to feel self-conscious of his clothing. The people there were not rich, but their clothes were not tattered or ill-fitting the way his were. It seemed as if he was constantly in someone's way and was moving too slowly for the general flow of traffic. His eyes finally spotted a vendor whose booth was set back far enough to the side that he felt confident he could stand there and make a purchase without being in anyone's way.

The vendor was a middle-aged woman who seemed quite harried and under pressure, even though Son was the only one shopping at her booth. "What are you doing here?" she asked him.

"I'm just passing through. I'm headed west," Son told her.

"Well, you should have left days ago," she said. "You'll never make it to the festival on time."

"What festival?" Son asked.

The woman just looked at him as if he was joking with her and asked, "Well, what do you want?"

Son sheepishly asked for a canteen, a loaf of bread, and a dozen medium-sized turnips. He wasn't very fond of turnips, but he didn't like the idea of fighting crowds to get roasted vegetables or grilled meat. Besides, he knew they would keep for a while, in case he didn't find another market anytime soon. He took his small jar of coins out and paid the woman, then made his way out of the busy street market with his eyes on the westwardly road that

17

led out of the village. It was even more of a challenge to navigate his way out of the crowd because the things he bought added more bulk to his pack and he would accidentally bump into other people with it.

Son finally made it back to the road. He tucked his walking stick under his arm, held the loaf of bread with one hand and a turnip in the other. Every time he took a bite of the turnip, he would take a bite of bread. He liked turnips even less than he remembered; luckily, the bread helped to cover the taste. It wasn't much, but it was brunch, and he had a long way to go.

CHAPTER THREE
THE MAN FROM THE NORTH

IT HAD BEEN A FEW days since Son had passed through the village where he'd bought the canteen, bread, and turnips. The bread was gone, and now he ate the vegetables with a generous amount of water. He was growing accustomed to camping every night. He would find a hidden spot off the road, make a fire, and sleep until just before daylight. Each day, he felt less sore and more rested. He would fill his canteen as often as possible, sometimes from a running creek, and sometimes kind strangers would give him water from their supplies.

He enjoyed observing the change in terrain as he walked. The roads were now a bit more straight and there were many more trees. Tall oaks were clustered together, separated by prairie grass that was as tall as he was. It made camping in secret much easier, since the farms were further apart and there were more places to hide.

It was early in the afternoon when Son noticed that he was down to his last turnip. He was partially relieved to almost be done with those horrible things, and partially worried that he may not find anything to eat for a while. After all, this part of the country was rather remote; he hadn't seen another village in days. Also, since it was so early in the season, there were no crops he could help himself to along the way.

Son could see a roadside tavern off in the distance. It wasn't the type of place he would normally visit, but he was almost out of food, and needed to fill his canteen. Miscreants, drunks, and ne'er-do-wells who were avoiding honest work and responsibility would occupy taverns like this day and night.

When Son was a little closer to the establishment he stood across the road from it, surveying the scene. There were two dirty-faced men sharing a bottle just outside the door, laughing drunkenly as they absentmindedly blocked the entrance. The boy could hear men talking loudly, arguing over working conditions, high rents, and whose belch was the most potent. There were only four or five horses hitched to the post, which was interesting to Son since there were so many people inside.

He didn't want to go in. He wondered if he should just keep walking, hoping he'd find something else soon. The chances were slim, though, so Son decided to gather his courage, try to look strong, and cross the road to the tavern.

He puffed out his chest, broadened his shoulders, leaned his walking stick against a tree, and headed toward the entrance. When he realized he wouldn't be able to enter until the two drunks moved out of the way, he respectfully said, "Excuse me, sirs."

The two men just kept talking loudly to each other, occasionally passing the bottle or giving each other a playful shove, so Son spoke louder. "Excuse me, sirs!"

They stopped what they were doing and looked at Son

as if he were being incredibly rude. Then one of the men got in Son's face. His breath reeked of whiskey. He stuck his finger in Son's chest, saying, "What are you lookin' at, ragamuffin?" and the two men laughed hysterically, as if it was the funniest thing either of them had ever heard.

Finally, after an unusual amount of time was spent laughing at Son's expense, the dirty-faced man nearest the door said, "We're just playing with you, little man. Go on in," and he motioned with his hand for the boy to pass by.

As Son entered the tavern, he was immediately confronted by the smell. It was a combination of drink, smoke, and sweat. It reminded him of the way his father smelled. For a moment, he was lost in conflicting emotions and memories as the scent seemed to transport him to times of comfort and sadness, pain and relief. It wasn't long ago that he'd heard his father say, "I don't like you, Son," and the sting of those words seemed to make its way up from wherever it was hidden in his heart.

Soon enough he was woken from his transfixion. Once inside the pub, one of the drunken men who'd blocked the entrance from the outside slammed the door hard behind Son and laughed far louder and longer than the action warranted. Now feeling somewhat trapped and insecure, Son began to wonder if stopping here was such a good idea after all.

Standing near the entrance, the boy could see a long counter to the right of the room. Behind the bar counter was an overweight barkeep with scraggly sideburns and an ineffective comb-over. He wore a dirty green apron over his clothes and walked with a limp. Despite his disheveled appearance, he still carried a rugged demeanor and moved at a moderate, intentional pace, even though there was a continual flow of beer orders being called out. There were stools along the bar, but few were being used as men stood around talking, arguing, and guffawing in the smoky tavern.

To Son's left there were a handful of tables. They were less occupied than the bar. Most of the men who sat at them sat alone or with one other person. They also seemed to be different from the men at the bar. Son guessed that the men at the tables were travelers from other parts of the country, just passing through.

Sitting alone at one of the tables was a man from the north. Son had never seen anyone from the north before, but he'd heard his father talk about them. Even though the man was sitting, Son could tell he was the tallest person in the tavern. He was light-skinned with thick, wavy black hair that looked like it had been groomed with an axe. His upper lip and chin hair was full, but the remainder of his beard didn't seem to grow in with the same plentitude. The man wore a long, dark fur coat, which Son thought was strange for this time of year. There was an empty plate on his table and he was quietly drinking a large stein of black stout.

Watching the man reminded Son of how thirsty he was, so he approached the counter to see if he could get some water. He pulled the leather canteen from his bag, uncorked it, and asked the barkeep if he would fill it for him.

"That'll be five cents," the barkeep said while drying the inside of a mug.

Shocked, Son replied, "Five cents? For water?"

"Do you want it or don't you?" the barkeep retorted in an irritated tone.

Feeling unsure about whether or not he was being cheated, Son took the jar of coins from his bag and gave the man five cents. Without saying a word, the barkeep filled the canteen from a bucket of clean water and handed it back to him.

Son decided he would rather not stay for dinner. After all, eating the last turnip seemed like a better idea than being in this place any longer than he had to be, so he put the canteen back in his bag, grabbed his jar of coins, and headed back toward the door.

As Son approached the door, a man quickly stepped in front of him and turned to block him from leaving the tavern. He was slightly overweight, had a wispy, dark-blonde mustache, and wore a brown vest and a small leather coif hat that rested just below his ears. He inhaled deeply from a cigarette and while exhaling asked, "Why don't you let me hold that jar of coins for you?"

Taking the question literally, Son said, "Thank you, but I don't need any help," and began to walk closer to the door.

Not moving out of the way, the man replied, "You're a little witling, aren't you?"

"No, sir. I just meant that—" Son started to reply before the man cut him off.

"I don't care what you meant!" the man growled in Son's face, then grabbed the jar.

Son's thoughts quickly filled with the worst-case scenarios that could happen without that jar of money. Something erupted inside of his mind and, out of anger and panic, he yelled, "Give that back or I'll tear your face off!"

Shocked by the boy's threat, the man asked, "What did you just say?" as his jaw tightened and his eyes fixed intently on Son's.

"I said give it back!" Son asserted with uncharacteristic boldness.

The man leaned in, close and intimidating, and said, "Or you'll rip my face off?"

Son paused for a second, realizing his threat may have not been the wisest choice of words. He eked out, "I... just... uh—" just before being interrupted.

"I want to see you try and rip my face off!" the man said, beginning to shove Son backward. "Do it!" he shouted as he gave Son a hard push into the tables.

He stumbled back, barely able to stay on his feet, until he caught himself on the table where the man from the north was sitting. He looked up and saw the thief walking out the door with his jar of coins and started after him. Unfortunately, his bag became snagged on the corner of the table, lifting it just enough to cause all that was resting on it (including the beer) to slide off.

Incredulous, the man from the north sprang to his feet and began yelling at Son in a language that was unfamiliar to him.

"I didn't mean to—" Son began to say.

"You didn't mean to what?" the man asked angrily in

the common language, and he drew a very large sword from a sheath that was hidden by his long fur coat.

Son was so stunned by the appearance of the sword that he didn't know what to say. He just stood there, shaking.

The man from the north now leveled his sword with Son's neck and asked again, "You didn't mean to what?"

"S-s-spill your beer," Son answered.

The man from the north replied, "I've killed men for less than that," and continued to hold his sword close to the boy's neck.

Perhaps it was the hunger and fatigue. Maybe it was the stress of the months that had led up to this moment. Or it could have been the helplessness and anger of having his money stolen. But Son's face turned red, and he yelled out at the top of his lungs, "THEN DO IT!!"

The man from the north's cool, angry demeanor broke as he wrinkled his forehead and asked, "What?"

Son yelled, "Do it! I want to die!" Tears started to jog down his cheeks.

Something about the boy's response tickled the man and he wasn't quite sure why. At first, a smirk crossed his face, then it turned into a smile, followed by an immediate and hearty belly laugh and he couldn't hold his sword up to Son's neck any longer.

The laughing only infuriated Son. Instead of taking the opportunity that presented itself in the break of tension, he unwisely took the old kitchen knife from his bag, held it up threateningly, and yelled, "Stop laughing at me!"

The man from the north regained his composure and, with no effort whatsoever, he rapped Son's hand with the broad side of his sword, causing him to drop the knife to the floor.

"Ouch!" Son yelled, and the two of them stood there looking at each other for a moment.

The man from the north then bent down, picked up the old knife, handed it to Son, and said, "I think it's time you were on your way."

Son was surprised by the gesture, and realized it would be best if he did as the man said. He placed the knife back in his bag and began walking towards the door again. He rubbed his sore hand, and as his adrenaline slowly subsided, he felt as if all of the strength had left his body.

All he wanted was to get back to the rhythm of the road, find a place to hide, and make a camp for the night.

CHAPTER FOUR
A BLESSED CURSE

As Son walked west along the road, he could only think about putting as much distance as possible between himself and the tavern before it became too dark. His knees felt weak, his head seemed to be spinning, and his stomach felt uneasy from the confrontation with the two men. Even though he was hungry, he didn't feel like eating.

As he walked, he cried. Tears rolled down his cheeks as he thought about having his money stolen and about the encounter with the man from the north.

A cold wind had kicked up, but Son paid no attention to it. His bag was slung over his shoulder, his walking stick was in his hand, and his teary eyes were fixed on the ground as he walked.

Son was so focused on the road beneath his feet that he didn't even notice the road in front of him. Nor did he notice the three men standing there waiting for him until he was upon them. Startled, he looked at them and gasped.

It was the man who'd stolen his jar of coins, and the two drunkards who were in front of the door when Son entered the bar. They didn't seem quite so slap-happy now as the three of them stood there.

"Hello, little witling," the thief said through his greasy, poor excuse of a mustache.

Son just stood there, frozen. He was trembling, afraid that this might be the end for him. He had no fight left in him, and he was too weak and hungry to try to run away. He managed to speak up and ask, "What do you want from me?"

"We're here to teach you a lesson, you little cretin," the man said as his companions grinned drunkenly.

Before Son had a chance to react, the man grabbed the boy and pulled him to the ground. When Son struggled, the man called for his friends to hold his arms down. Then the attacker rolled up Son's left sleeve as high as it would go.

"Now, we wouldn't want you to forget your lesson anytime soon, so I'm going to give you a little present," the man said as he took a deep drag from his cigarette and slowly let the red-hot ember sink into Son's arm.

Son cried out in pain as his skin burned from the cigarette. Three more times, the man inhaled from his cigarette and burned the boy's arm.

Then he growled, "You said you were going to rip my face off. I'm afraid *you're* the one who will be losing his face today." He pulled a flask of whiskey from his pocket and emptied its contents onto Son's face and hair. It burned Son's eyes, and he screamed and struggled as the other two men held him down.

At that moment, Son wished with everything he had that he would have stayed on the farm. All that was happening to him seemed surreal, and he couldn't believe people could be so cruel. He wished his father was there with him. He may not have been a very nice man, but he would have protected him. He would not have allowed men like this to treat him this way.

Through his tears, Son could see the man inhale deeply from his cigarette and begin to lower it towards his face. Son closed his eyes, knowing he was going to be in excruciating pain, but the burning never came. Instead, he heard the sound of a quick swoosh, and a thud. Then he felt the full weight of the man on top of him.

Son opened his eyes to discover that someone had forcefully thrown a beer stein at the man's head, and now he was laying unconscious on top of him. The cigarette was sandwiched between Son's chest and the thug from the tavern. He could feel the butt growing hotter. He realized that his hands were no longer being held down, so he wedged his right hand in between them, pulled out the cigarette, and threw it as far as he could.

When he threw the cigarette, he could see someone manhandling the two drunkards as if they were mere scarecrows. It was the man from the north. He first threw one of the men against a large tree and, while the man was still stunned, he threw the other man against him, knocking consciousness out of both of the drunkards.

Son couldn't believe what he was seeing! He was afraid he would be the man's next victim if he didn't get out from underneath his unconscious tormentor.

Then he saw the man from the north coming straight towards him. He pushed and struggled to free himself with great urgency, but to no avail. The tall, muscular man grabbed the thief by the belt and lifted him in the air as if he were a child. He grabbed the jar of coins from inside the man's vest and tossed him aside like a sack of wheat.

Son was unable to move. He was in awe of the enormity and strength the northerner possessed. The man retrieved a rag from inside his long, furry coat, took to one knee, and handed the rag to Son. "Use this to wipe off your face," he said. "And you might need this to get where you're going," he continued, as he handed Son the jar of coins.

"I don't understand," Son said as he slowly got to his feet, wiping away the whiskey from his face and hair. "Why did you help me?"

"Help you?" the man from the north asked indignantly. "I was denying you your wish."

"My wish?" Son asked, not understanding what he was talking about.

"In the tavern, you wished to die. Since you robbed me of my wish to enjoy a cold ale, I am robbing you of your wish to pass to the next life," the northerner explained.

Son didn't understand the man from the north's reasoning. Perhaps that was how his people avenged themselves, or perhaps his mind was touched. Whatever the reason, he was grateful for the man's help, even though he didn't fully trust him.

Then it occurred to Son that he still had a long way to go, and a guardian would sure be helpful on his journey. He picked up his walking stick, repositioned his bag on his shoulder, then said, "Well, you got me, sir. I guess I'll just have to end my life when I get further down the road.

It's getting dark. Maybe I'll trip and break my neck while I find a place to camp for the night."

"You will not get away with it that easily, boy!" the man declared. "I shall accompany you until I feel you have paid retribution for your offense."

"I suppose I deserve that, after what I did in the tavern," Son said. "I'm going to continue west until I find a place to camp for the night." Then he walked down the road, suppressing a smile as the man from the north followed a few paces behind.

It wasn't long before Son and the man from the north were some distance from the three tavern patrons. The sky was growing darker. Son was anxious to put the day behind him, even though he now had a complete stranger traveling with him.

A light rain started to fall, which wouldn't have bothered Son except for the cold wind that was blowing along with it. He pointed out an outcrop of tall, flat rocks to the south of the road. The rocks looked like they had been standing there for quite some time. They were gray, and mostly covered with moss. They leaned toward the south and would provide excellent protection from the rain and wind, as well as hide them from any other people traveling along the road.

Son quickened his pace and jogged through the field to the rocks while the man from the north continued to move at an even, deliberate pace. When they arrived, Son quickly built a fire, which he was becoming quite proficient at after several nights on the road. He sat down beside it, grateful for its warmth and for the shelter provided by the rocks. The man from the north sat on the opposite side of the small fire, his legs crossed and back straight.

As Son relaxed, the awareness of his hunger returned. He reached into his bag to take out the last turnip and his canteen. He took a long drink from the canteen, then began eating the turnip as if it were a delicious meal. After a day like today, even a turnip was a welcome treat.

After eating the entire thing and drinking about half of his water, Son realized that neither himself nor the man from the north had said a word to each other since leaving the road. Son wasn't very comfortable with silence when he was around others, but he was intimated by the man, and feared accidentally provoking him to anger. After all, the man was from the north. The people there had a reputation for quick tempers and violence.

Unexpectedly, it was the man from the north who broke the silence. "What is your name?" the man asked.

Taken a little off guard, Son wiped off his wet chin and answered, "Son."

"Son?!" the man replied, as if it were the most ridiculous name he'd ever heard. "Son is not a name. It's a title or a position, but it's not a name."

"Well, it's MY name," Son answered back. "It may not be much, but it's what I'm called."

"Your name is your birthright," the man from the north said. "It shapes your destiny and empowers your actions. Are you sure you do not have another?"

Feeling embarrassed and uncomfortable, Son attempted to steer the attention away from himself. "That is the only one I have. What is your name?"

It worked. With great pride, the man from the north

answered, "My name is Dulnear. In the northern tongue it means 'overcomer of great strength.' My father gave me this name and it has guided my path through life."

Son pondered the idea that a name could be so powerful. He wished that his own name had more meaning to it. He also admired the name Dulnear, and the images of courage and power it conjured in his mind. He asked, "May I call you by Dulnear?"

"Of course you can," the man answered. "It is an honor to be addressed by that name."

Son began to say, "Well, Mister Dulnear—"

"Just Dulnear, please," the man from the north interrupted.

"I'm sorry. Dulnear. I just wanted to say thank you for saving me from those men."

The man from the north replied, "You are a funny creature. You say that you want to die and then you thank me for saving your life."

Son, not wanting to lose the protection of his strange guardian, said, "Well, I just wasn't fond of the idea of having my face burned off."

"Ah, I see," said Dulnear. "You want to look your best at your home-going ceremony. I understand now."

Son simply nodded in agreement and said nothing else about the matter.

The two of them sat there for a while longer as the night settled in and the rain ceased. Eventually, Son decided to change his position so that he could sleep. He took the blanket from his bag, curled on his side, faced the fire, and tried to cover himself with the inadequate bedding he'd taken from his father's farm. Since the blanket was only long enough to cover Son from his shoulders to his knees, he had to coil himself up extra tight to get underneath it.

Looking at Son seemed to amuse the man from the north. He watched him struggle for a while, with a small grin on his face, before removing the bag that was slung across his chest and laying down himself. He laid on his back facing away from the rocks and closed up his long fur coat, leaving an opening just above his waist where his sword could be accessed. As he laid there drifting off, his hand rested on the hilt of his sword and he would often tighten his grip around it or swipe his thumb across the pommel.

Watching him, the boy wondered about all of the battles he must have fought, and all of the men he might have killed with his enormous sword. He still didn't know if he could trust him, but he was certain that he would rather have the man fighting for him than against him.

Son laid there thinking about the events of the day. He thought about how, just that morning, he was traveling alone, but now he had a strange companion. He pondered how he might have handled the experience in the tavern differently. He was also extremely grateful that he was rescued from those horrible men on the road. As he thought, his eyes grew heavier and his breaths grew deeper, until he drifted off into a light sleep next to the fire.

The man from the north laid there with his hand on his sword. He was used to living at a high level of alertness. Tuas-Arum was his homeland, where violence and bloodshed were a way of life. He had only been gone from his home for a few days before he happened to visit the tavern.

Dulnear was a violent man with a quick temper, even though those characteristics were distasteful to him. He hoped that, by leaving the north, he could change. But transforming one's nature doesn't come easily. It only took a spilled beer to initiate the kyu-ras, a petty northern custom of retribution.

He didn't know where he was going when he left the north, so following the boy made no interruptions to his plans. There was something about Son that the man couldn't quite put his finger on. Though they could not have been more different, he saw a vague shadow of himself in the boy. As he pondered the idea, he felt glad that he had saved him, and wondered if their meeting was more than chance.

———◆◆◆———

Sometime in the night, Son woke up because he had become uncovered from his inadequate blanket and was now shivering. It was very dark and quiet, and the only light he had was from the glowing remains of the dying fire. He was tired, and wanted to close his eyes to go back to sleep, but the silence made him uneasy.

When he'd fallen asleep earlier, the man from the north was lying nearby, going to sleep for the night, but now Son couldn't hear a sound. There was no snoring, no heavy breathing, no shifting or turning. For a moment, he was afraid that he was all alone again. He sat up and squinted towards the direction where he thought his companion was laying. Eventually, he was just able to make out a small section of Dulnear's heavy fur coat.

Relieved, Son laid down again and closed his eyes. As he laid there, he thought about how the man slept more quietly than anyone he'd ever seen before. He even wondered if he was sleeping at all. Most people made at least a little noise while sleeping, but not this man. He slept with incredible peace. He seemed to have no wants; no anxiety or fear. It was the complete opposite from the way the boy's father slept.

Son wondered what it would be like to have that kind of stillness in his thoughts. For as long as he could remember, he'd been anxious or afraid about something. Wherever he was, he wished he was someplace else. Whatever he was doing, he thought about other activities he'd rather be engaged in. Contentment and peace were seldom found by him, and he wished that he had even a small portion of what Dulnear seemed to possess.

It was a mystery to Son how a man from such a violent people could sleep so peacefully; that a warrior who lost his temper over spilled beer could sleep the whole night through without even a change in position.

He imagined being more like the sleeping giant, strong and confident, with no apparent care for provision or defense. He envisioned how differently things would have gone with the three men from the tavern if he were taller, stronger, or could wield a sword. He pictured himself wearing a long fur coat and drawing a massive sword out from underneath it, to everyone's horror and dismay. This version of him would have run all three men through at the same time while quipping, "Looks like it's shish kebab for dinner tonight!" and laughing maniacally.

Son smiled as the scenario played out in his mind, but it didn't last long. He soon thought about how powerless he was. How he wished he wasn't so small, so scared, and so helpless, even when he tried to stand up for himself. He wished for more security, more courage, and more strength, and he wished that he wasn't always wishing for something.

Soon Son wished himself back to sleep and, as he slept, he dreamed of returning home and seeing his mother once again.

In the morning, Son woke to the smell of coffee warming over a fire. Dulnear was already awake and was pouring some into a tin cup. The man sat with his legs crossed, sipping from the cup, and reading from an old book. It surprised Son to see a man of war reading. He assumed that, because of his brutish appearance, he was not a learned man.

Sitting up, Son sleepily asked, "You know how to read?"

"Of course I read!" Dulnear replied indignantly. "Don't you?"

"No. I'm afraid no one has ever taught me," Son answered.

"Then teach yourself," the man answered back. "Acquiring skill is your own responsibility. Never blame others for your lack."

Dulnear's sharp responses were off-putting to Son, but

he decided that he would not withdraw. He knew there was more to the man from the north than met the eye. He may have been quick-tempered and tactless, but the boy sensed a depth to him that he was drawn to explore.

Son stood up, stretched, and gathered his few things so he could begin his day of traveling. As he did, Dulnear followed suit. They put out the fire and started walking towards the road.

The sky wasn't fully lit yet, and the clouds seemed a little darker than usual. Son stared at the texture of the low-hanging heavens as he walked and mused once again about what it would be like to have fighting skills like the man from the north. Finally, it occurred to him that he could ask the man to teach him. The problem was that he didn't know how to ask. He was afraid that if he framed the question the wrong way, Dulnear would be angry, and he didn't want to provoke his short temper.

Just as they were reaching the road, Son realized how he could make his request. "Excuse me, Mister Dulnear," he said.

"Just Dulnear," the man corrected the boy.

"Sorry. Dulnear," Son responded, and said, "I was thinking about my punishment, and was wondering if it might honor my penance if I was better able to defend myself. I thought that, if you could teach me some of your fighting skills, it might lift the burden of reprisal you must carry towards me."

Dulnear, walking a couple of paces behind Son, could scarce hold back an amused smile as he saw through Son's attempt to ask for fighting lessons. He admired the lad's cleverness and asked, "So you want to learn the way of the warrior, do you?"

"Well, yes. I wouldn't want to be unexpectedly overtaken by bandits or run through by a ravager," Son answered.

"I see," said Dulnear, as the two of them walked westward along the road.

As minutes went by without a clear answer, Son started to feel impatient. He was hoping for an enthusiastic yes. Instead, he was left wondering with an, "I see." He wanted so badly to ask again. It was his tendency to repeat himself when he became anxious, but he resisted the temptation and walked in silence as he waited for an answer.

Finally, the man from the north said, "I will teach you the way of the warrior."

Containing his excitement the best he could, Son said, "That's great! This will really help with my punishment. Should we start with swords? Or perhaps I should learn hand-to-hand combat first. I just really want to make sure I don't die before my time."

There was a short pause before Dulnear answered, then he said, "You will start by learning to read."

That was not the response Son was hoping for, but he knew better than to argue with the man. The two of them continued to walk along the road as the morning moved on.

CHAPTER FIVE

The Tismatayed

IT WAS APPROACHING LATE AFTERNOON after Son's first night camping with the man from the north. They had walked for most of the day without stopping, eating, or saying much to each other. It was awkward for the boy to travel with a companion yet have so little communication happening between them. He wanted to fill the silence somehow, but was uncertain about what to say.

In the distance, Son saw a large village. He felt relieved that he would be able to purchase some rations, and maybe a weapon. He asked Dulnear, "There's a town ahead. Can we stop?"

"It is your journey," the man answered.

Son felt a little silly for assuming Dulnear into a parental role, even if it was just for a moment. "We will stop there for supplies," he said, trying to undo his assumption with the tone of his voice.

As they approached the village, Son noticed that there seemed to be many more people there than would have been typical for its size. There was music playing and vendors stationed up and down the street. People were dancing and feasting, and the smell of roast lamb and pheasant filled the air. He realized that this must be the festival the woman spoke of when he'd purchased his canteen and turnips.

A boyish excitement rose up in Son as he and Dulnear entered the town. His eyes darted back and forth to all of the street vendors' items on display. He thought about his jar of coins and wondered what he could buy with it. In fact, he was so preoccupied with all of the excitement that he didn't notice the strange looks he and the man from the north were getting. They were an unusual pair, this raggedy boy and his gigantic, fur-clad companion.

It didn't take very long for Son to find what he was looking for. It was a blacksmith with a large weapons display in the street outside of his shop. It wasn't too crowded around all of the swords, knives, sabers, and daggers, and he was more than happy to peruse all of them without the interference of trying to navigate a crowd. As he did, the man from the north followed just a step or two behind, occasionally looking down at the weapons, but generally uninterested.

Eventually, Son came upon a sword he felt would do the job for him. The weapon was the perfect size for his smaller-than-average hand. It was a broadsword with a smooth, somewhat dull blade and a leather-wrapped grip. The price of the weapon was equal to his entire jar of coins. He held the sword and gave it a few short swings through the air as he imagined what it would be like to face off with an attacker while wielding it.

Son thought it would be a good idea to ask for Dulnear's opinion before making the purchase. After all, if he was going to be his teacher, he should have some helpful advice on the right weapon to choose. "What do you think of this sword?" the boy asked.

The man from the north held the sword up and closely examined it, checking the weight, balance, and action. He then carefully handed it back to Son and said, "Perhaps you can trade your blanket for it."

Son paused and thought about Dulnear's statement. He felt foolish for being so zealous to buy a sword, but knew the man was right. He needed other things much more than he needed a sword. He put the weapon back where he found it and, without saying anything, headed towards the other street vendors to find supplies he needed for the rest of his trip.

As they walked deeper into the village, Son found it difficult to find what he was looking for because of the throng of people moving in every direction. There were shops and sellers that he wanted to browse but felt uncomfortable because of the congestion. However, he did notice that people seemed to move out of the way when they saw Dulnear coming, so he tried not to walk too far ahead of him.

Eventually, he found a vendor that sold supplies for travelers. There were tents, lanterns, and skillets, but without a mule or horse, Son knew it wouldn't be wise to try and carry too much. He found a new blanket that he could afford. It was large enough to cover him comfortably and could be rolled up and slung over his shoulder with a bit of twine. It was brand-new and still smelled of freshly spun wool, and was dark gray with hemmed edges. In a way, Son wished it was nighttime already so that he could huddle under it and enjoy its warmth.

He also found a proper hunting knife. It had a spear-shaped blade that was sharpened on both sides, and a polished wooden handle. It wasn't as ornate or impressive as other knives being sold, but it felt like the right one for Son. The two items together cost him over half of his money, but he believed it was a wise investment for the long journey to return to his mother.

Son was getting weary of the crowds and wanted to start making his way out of the village, but thought it would be best to have a decent meal before leaving. He purchased a large plate of lamb with potatoes and carrots and sat down at one of the many tables set out for the festival. The man from the north did the same, with the addition of a large stein of dark, stout beer.

The two didn't say much to each other, but Son didn't mind. He was eating the best meal he'd had since he could remember. He devoured the meat as if each bite contained the taste and smell of ten meals. By the time he reached the end of his plate, his stomach was full. It was a feeling he hadn't experienced since the days when he lived with his mother.

Son was feeling exceptionally positive this early evening. His hunger was satisfied, and he was the owner of a brand-new blanket and knife. He had never owned anything brand-new before. His clothes were hand-me-downs, and he'd made most of his personal items himself.

It felt good to have new things; it gave him a sense of confidence.

As he sat waiting for Dulnear to finish his beer, he noticed a book vendor nearby and walked over to talk to the proprietor. He was a kindly looking, white-haired old man wearing a pair of reading glasses. "Do you have any books for people who can't read?" the boy asked curiously.

"Do you mean for lads just learning?" the vendor asked in return.

"Yes, sir. I want to learn how, but I don't know where to start," Son said.

The man pulled a medium-sized book from a shelf, opened it up so Son could see its contents, and said, "This is what you're looking for then. It's called a reader. It illustrates the sound of each letter with a picture, then has several pictures with the corresponding words written next to them."

"I see. How much is it?" Son asked.

"It's fifty cents," the old man answered.

When Son heard the price he was disappointed, because he only had forty-five cents remaining in his jar. But since he was feeling confident and full, he decided to try something. He took the book, as if to examine it carefully, and stared for a few seconds at the first and last pages. He then looked up at the book vendor and asked, "Why are there blank pages at the end of the book?"

"Because all books have an even number of pages in them," the man explained. "If the written material fills up an odd number, then it leaves a couple of empty pages at the end."

Son paused for a second and said, "Well, I don't think

I can pay for pages with nothing on them. Will you take forty-five cents for it?"

The man had a feeling Son was short on money but wanted him to have the book. He said, "I'll tell you what; promise me that you'll read it every day and I'll give it to you for thirty cents."

"It's a deal!" Son said with a big smile on his face. He took thirty cents from his jar and handed it to the man. He then took the book, placed it in his bag, and headed back to where Dulnear was still seated enjoying the last swig of his beer.

As Son and the man from the north walked westward, away from the town, they moved a little slower than usual. They had covered many miles already, and were full and satisfied from their lamb and vegetables. It was getting darker, but there was still time to go a little further before it was too dark to find a place to camp.

As they walked, Son decided to show Dulnear his new knife. He wasn't overly excited about doing so after getting the man's opinion of the sword he was interested in buying, but was genuinely interested in what he had to say.

"Would you look at my knife for me?" Son asked politely. He withdrew it from his bag and held it out to the man, handle first.

Dulnear took the knife from Son, stopped walking, and closely examined it. After looking at it for a few seconds, he reached into his bag and withdrew an old, worn sheath and a length of leather string. He fastened the string to the sheath, placed the knife inside of it, and handed it to Son, saying, "Wear this under your coat. You'll want to be able to access it quickly, but you don't want others to know you have it."

Somewhat stunned by the man's kind gesture, the boy quickly removed the bag from over his shoulder, took off his coat, and slipped his head and arm through the string so that the knife was hanging next to his ribs. He put the old coat back on and slung his bag back across his chest, but could feel the knife resting securely underneath. As he felt it there, he experienced something new to him. It was a feeling of security. He had a concealed knife and, even though it was a hunting knife, he could use it to protect himself if he needed to. "Thank you," Son said, and though the man from the north never said what he thought of the knife, he knew that he approved.

"If you have to go fumbling through your bag when you need it, you'll only end up eating more turnips," Dulnear said with a subtle grin, and the two resumed walking down the road.

Son was happy. He was the owner of a fine knife, a new blanket, and a book. He was also traveling with the closest thing he'd ever had to a friend, even if he didn't say much, and was technically punishing Son for offending him. It was the grandest day ever, and the boy let himself feel good about it.

It was soon time to veer off of the road to find a place to camp for the night. Son and Dulnear headed south through a wide, grassy prairie, and decided to walk a little further than usual since there was very little brush or rock for them to use as cover. After hiking for a while, they noticed a strange sound coming from somewhere in the distance. It was the sound of men chanting. The low, droning chorus sent shivers down the boy's back.

Son and Dulnear stood and looked at each other for a moment. Then the man from the north, with a serious expression on his face, said, "We should take a closer look."

Those weren't exactly the words Son was hoping to hear, and his heart began to beat faster as he considered the terrain and the rapidly darkening sky.

Dulnear began to move through the prairie grass as he headed in the direction of the chanting. Son was impressed by how stealthily the man moved, given his size, and was focused on keeping up with him for fear of being left alone on the dark prairie amidst the eerie melody.

Soon they came upon a narrow, craggy valley. At the base, they could see two long rows of robed men carrying torches as they walked in a northerly direction. There were several dozens of them, and they were moving towards an immense stone that sat at the center of the valley.

Without saying a word, Son and Dulnear made their way to a small, rocky outcropping located just a spear's throw from the large stone. It gave them sufficient cover, as long as they remained crouching, and from there they could see clearly what was going on.

Being closer, Son now noticed that only half of the robed figures were men. The other half were boys like himself. Each pair, a boy and a man, would approach the stone. The boy would carve something into the stone, then the man would face the boy and place his hand on his shoulder. The man would speak a few words to the youth, then hand him a sword. When the boy took the sword, he would hold it over his head, and the whole crowd would stop chanting to yell and cheer. Son thought this was very strange and asked Dulnear, "What's happening here?"

"It is a Tismatayed," the man from the north said, "a rite of passage ritual. As the boy approaches the Athru stone, he carves his name onto it, symbolizing that he is giving it up to receive a new name. His father then speaks to the boy and bestows his own name upon him. From this day forward, the boy will be known by his father's name and the father will take on a new one. The ritual is concluded when the father gives his son a sword that was probably passed to him at his own Tismatayed."

Son understood now why there was a festival in the nearby village. It was a celebration of the father and son ritual in the valley. He was fascinated by the whole thing and watched intently as pair after pair approached the Athru and father imparted manhood onto son.

Fascination soon turned to irritation though, as Son realized that he would never have an experience like this. He saw the pride in the fathers' eyes, a look he had never seen in his own father's eyes, and the beaming excitement on the faces of the sons. He resented those looks, and began to think of criticisms about the way the boys held their swords and cheered. His thoughts accused the boys of being soft and arrogant. He imagined that they lived in nice houses and probably couldn't survive life on the road the way he had. He desperately fought off thoughts of being less than and unloved. Irritation gave way to sadness, and Son just wanted to leave.

"Let's go," Son said to Dulnear, and the two of them headed out of the valley. It was plenty dark now and they weren't sure where they were going, other than away from the sound of chanting and cheering. When it was quiet enough they stopped, and the man from the north crouched down and lit a small fire with some prairie grass. It gave him enough light to see that they were very close to some foliage they could use as cover while they slept for the night. He grabbed a small stick so he could transfer the fire to their campsite, and stoked it just large enough for them to get situated.

Son kept quiet and tried not to look at Dulnear because he didn't want him to see that he was crying. He curled up on his side and pulled his new blanket over himself. The smell of the newly spun wool was a comfort to Son, albeit a small one, and he thought about how such a wonderful day could turn into such a horrible one. He wondered if he would ever feel the way the boys looked at the ceremony. He wondered if he would always be just a ragamuffin, unimportant and inferior.

As the man from the north prepared a place to lay down for the night, he reminisced about his own Tismatayed. He thought it was strange that Son had no idea what it was, since it was a ritual practiced over the entirety of Aun.

His own manhood ceremony wasn't as orderly as the one he'd just witnessed. Unfortunately, in the north, it was common for fights to break out during public gatherings and festivals. That night was no exception. When a boy decided to carve his name into the Athru stone larger than the other names, a clash broke loose that started a clan war lasting several months. Another boy, when given a sword, swung it around with too much zeal and accidentally cut his own ear off. It was the only time Dulnear had seen someone injured, and he'd heard a collective sigh of relief from everyone around him. If the boy would have cut anyone else's ear off, a bloody battle would have ensued for sure.

What he remembered most was receiving his name. His father looked at him with such delight in his eyes as he imparted it to him. It was a moment that was branded onto the heart of the warrior forever. It was a long time ago, but he would never forget it.

CHAPTER SIX
Son and the Woodsmen

I T WAS EARLY IN THE morning and Son was sitting up, learning to read from his book. Nearby, Dulnear was reading as he sat sipping at his coffee. It had been three days' travel since the Tismatayed ceremony, and the landscape had changed from prairies and farmland to rugged forest. It made it easier to find places to camp without hiking so far off the road.

The two were finding somewhat of a rhythm to their days, carrying on with a morning routine, walking, establishing camp, and sleeping under the sky. Son even found himself taking on many of Dulnear's inclinations. He sipped coffee, when the man from the north was in the mood to share, and started sitting up with his legs crossed and his back straight, the same way Dulnear did.

Conversations were still a bit sparse. Dulnear wasn't much for small talk, but Son was becoming more at peace with long silences. Words seemed to be important to the man, and he used them much like silver coins. They carried weight, and weren't to be scattered about like barley seed. Dulnear was intentional when he talked, and the boy learned to think before he addressed him.

Morning was becoming Son's favorite part of the day. It was waking rest, a luxury seldom experienced for either of them. It was a time to learn to read, and a chance to take inventory and sort his belongings before the day's walk. Unfortunately, it wasn't a very long part of their day, since they had to be back on the road before the morning haze lifted.

As the two of them walked through the morning mist, Son heard a strange sound. It was like an elk bugling, but much deeper and muffled-sounding. It was eerie and made the boy uncomfortable. "What was that?" Son asked Dulnear.

"What was what?" Dulnear replied, and the deep howl repeated itself.

"That sound, it's so ghostly. Where is it coming from?" Son asked again as the sound persisted.

"I have no idea what you're talking about," Dulnear said with an irritated tone.

Surprised that the man from the north couldn't hear it, Son continued, "It's the most unusual thing I've ever heard. It's coming from right over..." he paused for a moment as he listened closely, "THERE!!" he shouted as he pointed directly at Dulnear's stomach. "It's coming from you!"

Dulnear stopped walking, looked a bit embarrassed, and said, "I am very hungry."

The two had had very little to eat over the last three days, and even though Son was feeling it, it was impacting Dulnear's extra-large frame much more.

The man from the north was an excellent forager, and Son would often watch to see what he harvested so that he could pick some for himself. However, after walking for long distances every day, the leaves and berries did almost nothing to satisfy their hunger.

"Can we hunt?" Son asked.

"I have been keeping my eyes fixed on finding game, but something has driven it from this area," Dulnear answered.

"Maybe it's the sound of your stomach," Son said jokingly as he let out a snicker.

Dulnear just looked at Son without saying a word.

The boy then said, "I'm sure we'll be coming to a village soon. We can buy some food."

"I have no money for food, and you are down to your last few cents," Dulnear said.

Son wasn't expecting to hear that. His assumption was that the man from the north was a person of means, since he read and carried a sword. He would never have guessed that he had no money. Feeling a bit panicked, the boy asked, "What will we do?"

"A solution will present itself," Dulnear answered confidently. "One always does."

And the two of them continued traveling the road west.

After walking into the early afternoon, the road they were traveling on eventually formed a wide ledge along a modest cliff. From there they could see quite a long distance. Looking out, Dulnear noticed many downed trees and a handful of shelters.

"Loggers. That explains the absence of wildlife," the

man from the north observed. "I think we've found a solution to our coin problem."

"Are we going to ask them for money?" Son asked.

"Of course not! We're going to work for it," Dulnear answered.

The boy didn't quite know what to think about that. He had never worked a job before. His only experience with labor was working on his father's farm, and that did very little to get him excited about visiting a logging camp.

They continued following the road west until it led them down to low, level ground. From there, they could see a wagon trail that led deep into the forest. They walked the trail until they came across a couple of men transporting logs toward the road on a horse-pulled cart. Son watched from a few steps behind as Dulnear approached them. He couldn't quite hear what he said, but he saw the two men point down the trail, deeper into the woods.

A few minutes later, they came to a large area where the trees had already been cut down. There were a few men cutting limbs off of downed trees, and others who were placing the trees on carts to be hauled off. Son and Dulnear walked through this area until they came to a place where the loggers were cutting down more trees. Men were chopping and yelling, and the whole thing just looked rather dangerous and chaotic to Son.

A man who looked like he was in charge was barking instructions at a couple of loggers when he saw Son and Dulnear standing nearby. He approached them and said, "You two can't be here. It's not safe for travelers."

"We're looking for work," Dulnear said. "Just an afternoon's worth."

The foreman looked at the two of them and said, "We could always use a couple of delimbers, but I'm not so sure about the wee lad."

"He'll do fine," the man from the north stated plainly. It may have been Dulnear's size and demeanor, but the foreman didn't argue with him.

The logger paused for just a moment and said, "Each of you grab an axe and head back that way. You'll be paid at the end of the day."

The two took axes from a nearby table covered with tools and headed back in the direction they came. As they did, they received ample stares from the other loggers. Most of them were rugged, hardworking men who seemed to enjoy what they did. Some of the laborers weren't so industrious though. They stood around complaining to each other, looking as though they weren't accustomed to such hard work.

When they came to a place where there were several felled trees that needed to be delimbed, the man from the north removed his large coat. When he did, there was a remarkable amount of clanging metal sound and it hit the ground with a heavy thud. He also removed his sword belt with its massive sword attached. It was the first time Son had seen the man without his coat. His arms were bare and muscular, and covered in scars. Son tried not to stare but it wasn't easy. He took off his own coat and bag and set them down next to Dulnear's. He felt strange that his knife was now exposed, but he was afraid that if he left it by his other things it would be stolen. The other loggers made him feel uneasy, and he found it difficult just to act naturally and work around them. He wished he could work in an area where no one could see him, but it was a wide-open space, and there was no privacy.

The man from the north, noticing that Son didn't know where to begin, pointed towards a downed tree and said, "You start on that one, and I'll start here."

"Okay," Son responded. Then he walked over to the tree Dulnear pointed at and began hacking the branches off of it. It wasn't as easy as he thought it would be. He placed one foot on the trunk of the tree, held the axe above his head, and repeatedly chopped downward on each limb until it came off. Quickly, he began to sweat and breathe heavily.

After Son had cut off two or three limbs, a nearby logger yelled, "Why don't you try swinging at it with your purse, little lady!" and all of the men within earshot burst into laughter.

Flustered and red-faced, Son looked over at Dulnear, who was already halfway through his second tree. He walked to the man and asked, "How did you get so far this quickly?"

The man from the north, looking contented as can be, replied, "Swinging an axe, the smell of trees, sweat. It brings life to my bones!"

Son had never seen anyone look so happy to be working so hard. His associations with labor had always been toil and criticism. He asked, "You actually enjoy this?"

"Of course I do!" Dulnear replied. "A true warrior takes pride in his work. It is not a drudgery to be endured, but an accomplishment that benefits oneself and others. If this opportunity doesn't suit you, then at least be thankful to the Great Father that he has given you able arms and legs to work and earn money for food."

Son said, "But my arms and legs aren't strong enough. I'm worn out after only a few limbs."

"That's because you're swinging that axe like a wild man," Dulnear began. "You won't last another hour like that. Watch me. Stand on the opposite side of the tree and keep both feet firmly on the ground. Make sure to keep your eye where you want the axe to land. Swing from the side, use the weight of the axe head, and chop," Dulnear said as he demonstrated for Son. "Now you try it."

Son chose a branch from the same tree and followed the man's instructions exactly. At his first swing, he cut a third of the way through the branch. He swung again and again, and the limb was completely removed. He couldn't believe how much easier it was. He smiled in relief, feeling like he was just given a magical tool to get the job done. "Thank you, Dulnear!" he said, and felt somewhat excited to get back over to his tree and resume his work.

After clearing his tree, and another, and yet another, the boy stopped to breathe in the forest air and thought about the man from the north's words. He decided that he would try to take pride in his work. He cleared each tree as he imagined a true warrior would and before he knew it, the afternoon was spent, and the foreman was bringing pay out to all of the workers. He looked at Son and complimented him on a job well done. "You did a fine job for a lad," the man said. "And any lack was more than made up for by your immense friend. Here is your pay. You earned it."

As he gave Son the handful of coins, the boy had to

force back a gleeful smile. He had never seen so much money before. It was more than his jar contained when he'd left his father's farm, and he began to imagine the things he could buy with it. As he stuffed it into his pocket, the man from the north approached them, and he received his pay as well.

Impressed by Dulnear's work, the foreman asked, "Would the two of you like to stay on and work for a few more days?"

"You'll have to ask the boy," Dulnear answered.

The man looked at Son and asked, "So how about it, lad? Would you like to earn some more money?"

Son was excited about the idea of having more money. He imagined himself buying a deadly sword, his own coffee pot, and maybe another book. Then he remembered why he was on this journey in the first place. It was to be reunited with his mother. He loved his mother more than books and swords, and wished that he could just snap his fingers and instantly be with her. "I'm sorry, but we must be going," he answered the man.

"Fair enough," the foreman replied. "But would you like to join the crew for dinner? You two look like you could use a bite to eat, and there's going to be a mighty feast in the mess tonight."

"I would like that very much. Thank you!" Son said, and he shook hands with the foreman and smiled a grateful, tired smile.

As the foreman went on his way to pay the other men, Son and Dulnear returned to their belongings. Son noticed that, as the man from the north put his money away, he put a couple of coins in one pocket, a couple in another, and the remainder in a pouch stored in his bag.

"Why do you keep your money like that?" Son asked.

"Some to spend, some to give, and some to save," Dulnear answered.

Son felt a little silly for keeping all of his money in a jar now and decided to put his money away the same way. The only difference was that he only had a jar instead of a leather pouch. He made a mental note that he should buy or make a pouch the next time he had the opportunity. Then he asked, "Are you hungry?"

"Enough to eat a mountain of turnips!" Dulnear said jokingly.

"Very funny," Son replied, and the two of them followed the flow of the other workers to the mess shelter.

The mess shelter was a large, rectangular tent. When they arrived there, it was filled with so many men that Son wondered if they would even get to eat any of the food that was set out. It was loud and full of commotion. There was a long table running down the center of the tent, and men were situating themselves in the chairs that surrounded the table. On the table, in front of each chair, was a wooden bowl and spoon.

In his ravenous state, Dulnear made his way straight to the table and took a chair, making deference to no one. Fortunately, there was a chair available next to him, and Son quickly sat down before anyone else had a chance to take it. Truth be told, most of the men were not interested in sitting next to the man from the north, as his large size and imposing demeanor intimidated even the hardiest of them.

When the foreman came in, he took the chair on the other side of Dulnear. "I'm glad you could join us," he said with a smile. "We'll eat in just a moment."

When everyone saw that the foreman was seated, it quieted down and the remaining chairs were taken. Some of the men had to stand, but they didn't seem to mind, and they were handed bowls and spoons to use as well. The foreman stood, placed his hand on his chest, and prayed over the meal, "Great Father, we thank thee for work, for providence, and for this meal. Amen."

When the man sat back down, the loggers frantically began filling their bowls with potatoes, carrots, roast beef, and bread. The flurry of arms and bowls made it difficult for Son to get any food, but he was too hungry to let timidity stop him. He just kept trying until he had enough food in his bowl to make a meal.

Dulnear had no difficulty filling his bowl, since the crewmen seemed to back away from whichever platter of food he was reaching for. When he was done serving himself, Son wondered how the man was able to pile the food in his bowl so high.

As the two were fully engaged in eating their dinner, Son had a strange suspicion that one of the men standing to the rear of the tent was watching him. At first he tried passing his suspicion off as paranoia, but he just couldn't shake the feeling. He tried to act nonchalantly, as if he was not aware that he was being stared at, but he knew he was doing a horrible job of it. He looked at his bowl and took a mouthful of bread. When he looked back up, to his disquiet, he found himself making eye contact with the man. He immediately looked away and pretended to be scanning the room for something. After a few seconds, he decided to look back at the man to see if he was still staring at him. He was. But, when Son saw him this time, he was filled with a fear that weighed him down, for he recognized the man. It was the man from the tavern who'd stolen his money and tried to burn his face.

The memory of that day rolled over the boy like a millstone, and he felt weak as he tried to continue eating with trembling hands. Terror held him in a vice so strongly that he didn't even think to inform Dulnear right away. He was frozen.

The man from the tavern, however, was thinking very clearly. He wanted to hurt Son, but he knew that wasn't going to happen while he was with Dulnear. Knowing a man from the north couldn't resist roughhousing, the shifty ne'er-do-well slyly tossed a potato at him. It seemed to come from nowhere and bounced off the large man's fur-clad chest. Immediately, Dulnear slammed his fist on the table and yelled, "Who threw that?!"

The potato thrower hunched down a bit and pointed to a group of men standing nearby.

Dulnear saw the pointing hand, followed its general direction, and threw the potato at one of the men in the group. It hit the man so hard that he was thrown back into another man. The second man's bowl ended up spilling its entire contents all over him. Infuriated, the second man picked up a handful of spilled food off of the ground and threw it in Dulnear's direction. Not only did some of the food hit Dulnear, but also the foreman and the man sitting next to him as well.

Immediately the shelter erupted with flying food, screaming men, tackles, and punches. It was total chaos. Son was doing his best to hide under the table and avoid the conflict. He winced every time a loud *Slam!* hit the table above him. He could hear Dulnear laugh as he fought with the other men. The boy doubted that the other men were having as much fun, and wondered how much of this skirmish was a good-natured brawl, and how much was men intentionally trying to injure each other. His wondering didn't last long though. He felt a tap on his shoulder and quickly looked behind him. It was the seedy man from the tavern.

The man covered Son's mouth with his hand and began dragging him out from underneath the table backward. The boy kicked and flailed and tried to yell for Dulnear, but to no avail. It was no problem at all for the man to take Son completely out of the shelter without anyone noticing.

When they were outside, a few feet away from the tent, the man lifted Son off of his feet and threw him to the ground. He yelled, "You're not so tough without the man from the north, are you!"

Son talked to himself inside his head. *Don't freeze. What are your options? Don't freeze!* He thought about drawing his knife but realized that, if the man disarmed him, things could go very badly. It was best if the man didn't know he had one. Finally, he decided to try to appease the man with an unexpected apology. "I'm sorry!" Son yelled. "Please forgive me, sir!"

The man was caught off guard for a second, then yelled, "You should be sorry, you dirty little vagrant!"

Son didn't know what he was apologizing for but it seemed to be working for the moment. He continued, "You're absolutely right, sir. I've been horrible."

The apology seemed to be losing its effectiveness and the man's anger rekindled. "You're bloody right you're horrible! And now you're going to get yours!" the man shouted as he began to kick Son's legs. Son crawled backward as quickly as he could, but the man continued kicking his legs until the boy was backed up against a tree.

The man stopped kicking Son for a moment and picked up a large stone. He held it above his head and said, "Now, you're going to give me the money you made today."

Son started to reach inside his bag for the money when he saw a large hunk of lamb fly through the air and hit the man squarely in the side of the face. It stunned the man for a moment and, by the time he realized what had happened, Dulnear was standing next to him.

Before the man could respond, the man from the north had him by the shirt with his left hand and was looking down at him. Caught by surprise, the spiteful man could only utter, "Why do you throw things at me?"

"'Twas a waste of a good roast," Dulnear responded, and he took a large bite of the lamb's leg he was holding with his free hand.

Son watched with a sense of delight and guilt. He was delighted to see such a horrible man handled so roughly, yet felt guilty for his delight. After all the man had done to the boy, he still didn't think it was right to enjoy watching him get his comeuppance.

Dulnear then took the leg of lamb he'd been eating and started slapping the man in the face with it, back and forth. The lowlife didn't try to defend himself. He must have known it would only enrage the man from the north further, so he endured, whimpering quietly.

"What should we do with this miscreant?" Dulnear asked.

Stifling a giggle from the sight of a grown man being slapped by a roast, Son said, "I don't know, but I don't want him following us."

"Then I shall pin him to the ground with a spear," Dulnear answered.

The man from the tavern looked terrified now as the roast slapping continued.

"I was thinking something less... bloody," Son said. It worried Son that he possessed such influence on the man from the north that it could lead to someone's impalement.

"I know then," Dulnear replied, and he laid one final smack against the man's head with the leg of lamb. This time, it was hard enough to knock the consciousness out of him. Dulnear then hoisted the man over his head and tossed him behind some nearby foliage, saying, "That should keep him out of your hair for now."

Son was shaken. He was also troubled by the words *for now*. He was afraid of future run-ins with the man from the tavern, but didn't know what to do. He hoped that he would complete his journey and that their paths would never cross again.

"I think it would be a good time for us to get out of here

and find a place to camp for the night," the boy expressed. He tried to get to his feet but struggled. The man's kicking had done more damage than Son initially realized.

Looking concerned, Dulnear held out his hand and helped the boy up. He asked, "Can you walk?"

Son tried taking a step or two but the pain on the outside of his left knee was so great that his leg buckled and he couldn't go any further. Grimacing from the pain, he looked at Dulnear and said, "I'm sorry."

The man from the north then grasped Son's arm and swung him onto his back. "Hold on, boy," he said. "I'll take care of the walking tonight."

Son had never ridden on someone's back before. He held onto Dulnear's shoulders while the large man provided support for his legs, being very careful with Son's injured knee.

It was a strange sensation being so high off the ground. As they made their way out of the logging camp, back toward the road, Son admired the strength and confidence of Dulnear. He was very thankful for his unusual friendship, and wondered if he would ever carry the same boldness and courage as the man from the north.

Dulnear moved hastily down the road with Son on his back. The boy wondered if the man from the north normally walked this fast, or if he was trying to travel as much distance as possible from the logging camp before it was completely dark. It was a cool, windy evening, and the boy was looking forward to resting his sore, tired body.

In the distance, Dulnear could see a ring of trees

surrounding a small clearing. He walked southwesterly off the road and swiftly headed for it. When they arrived, he carefully set Son down on a soft patch of grass and began building a fire. Son took the bag and blanket off of his shoulder and laid them down next to him. He leaned back, propped up on his elbows, and watched the man work quickly as the last remains of light faded from the sky.

When Dulnear was satisfied with the fire, he checked up on Son. "How is that leg?" he asked compassionately.

"It still hurts," Son answered, surprised by the caring nature of the man from the north. "Thank you for saving me… again," he added.

Dulnear paused and, with kindness in his eyes, asked, "You really don't want to die, do you?"

"I guess not. But I'm afraid that I'll never truly live, either," Son replied.

"What do you mean?" Dulnear pressed.

"I'm just a peasant. I don't have anything of worth, and my own family doesn't even want me," Son confessed as he looked at the fire.

Dulnear gently took Son's chin and shifted his head so that they were eye to eye again and asked, "Why are you on the road?"

Son's composure began to weaken and a tear ran down his cheek as he explained, "My father abandoned me at the farm, so I am traveling to find my mother." Then he cried some more as he told the man from the north about his mother's illness, his uncle Kione, and the difficult time he'd spent living with his father.

When Son's story was done and the tears had subsided,

Dulnear continued to look at Son and said, "It takes heat and pressure to turn a lump of coal into a diamond." He then took Son's blanket and laid it across the boy, saying, "You must be growing into something very special."

Son had never heard words like these from a man before, much less one whom he admired, like the man from the north. They felt good, like medicine to his soul. He imagined what kind of man he would be when he grew older, and hoped with all of his heart that he really would be something special.

As Dulnear got up to make a place to sleep, he had one last question for Son. He said, "I've been meaning to ask you something. Why did you buy a saddle blanket?"

"A what?" Son replied.

"Your blanket. It was made for a horse's back," the man explained.

Son closed his eyes for a moment, wondering if he'd ever get anything right, then something happened. He laughed. He didn't know why, but his discouragement turned to amusement, and he laughed harder and harder until his side ached. Dulnear laughed too, but with a tentativeness, like he didn't really know what they were laughing about. The boy's disappointment dissolved with the laughter, and he decided that he was glad he'd bought the blanket anyway. After all, it was warmer than his old one, and he could fit his entire body underneath it. "Goodnight, Dulnear," he said with a smile.

As Son laid back, heavy-eyed and sore, he gazed into the blackness of the night sky and thought about his day. He thought about working in the logging camp, the man from the tavern, and most of all, the kind words that

Dulnear had spoken to him. Just before drifting off, a strong breeze blew across their camp. Son wasn't sure, but he thought he saw a light in the sky. Briefly, the clouds were pushed eastward, and the sky above them was revealed. Directly above the boy were three stars shining brightly. Son couldn't believe what he was seeing, but before he could call attention to them, the clouds concealed them once again. It wasn't long after that when Son's fatigue overtook him, and he slept deeply through the night.

Dulnear laid there awake for quite some time. He was concerned for Son and the injuries to his legs. The thought of someone abusing the boy made him furious. He imagined all of the ways he could inflict pain upon the bully from the tavern.

There was something nagging at him though. He knew that fighting the boy's battles would do him no good, and simply teaching him how to fight the way he was trained as a lad may lead to Son becoming the bully. He had to do things differently.

Something rose up inside the man from the north that he had never experienced before. It was a sense of purpose, and he let it take root in his heart. He decided that he would teach the boy things that he should have learned from his father but didn't. Perhaps it would make a difference in Son's life. Dulnear stayed up for a while longer thinking about this, and praying to the Great Father for wisdom.

Very early the next morning, Son drowsily woke from his sleep. He opened his eyes, just a little, and could see Dulnear kneeling next to him. His hand was placed gently on the boy's knee, and he was whispering something in his native tongue. Son was so sleepy that he thought he might be dreaming. He quickly fell back asleep and didn't move until an hour later, when the sky was brighter.

When the boy awoke for the day, he looked over and saw the man from the north in his usual morning position, sitting up straight, drinking coffee, and reading from his book. It was a comfort to see him there, and he watched him do his routine for a few minutes before getting up.

As Son sat up, Dulnear asked, "How is your knee today, boy?"

Son bent and straightened his left leg a few times and answered, "Stiff, but much better." He stood up and walked around a bit, testing out his knee. He was amazed at how much better it felt, after not being able to put any weight on it the night before.

As the boy walked around the small clearing, he thought about the conversation he'd had with the man from the north the night before. He admitted that he really didn't want to die, and was afraid that Dulnear was going to leave him on his own, now that he knew his story. As he kept walking, he said, "Dulnear?"

"Yes?" Dulnear responded.

Son nervously asked, "I was wondering, would you like to accompany me to Blackcloth to find my mother?"

"Yes," Dulnear answered matter-of-factly.

Son kept walking. He was relieved and excited but was doing his best to match the man's stoic expression.

Then Dulnear said, "But I think we'll be staying off the road today. It would be a good day to learn some defense skills."

Son could hardly believe what he was hearing. It felt like ages since Dulnear had offered to teach him the ways of a warrior, and he was so delighted that he shouted, "Really?! This is incredible! Where do we start?"

Dulnear sat silently, looking at Son without an expression on his face, then said, "We start with you sitting down and being at peace. Everything else is dependent upon your ability to be still."

Son sat down, facing the man, with legs crossed and back straight, and tried to squelch a persistent smile that kept sneaking onto the corner of his mouth.

Dulnear's expression remained stoic and he began to instruct the boy. "This is not a matter to smile about. Impulsivity, lack of restraint, restlessness; these things will undo a great warrior. A man may have great fighting skills, but if he has not the right heart, he is a danger to himself and others."

Son took in what Dulnear was saying to him. He thought about how he'd impulsively yelled at the man from the tavern when he took the jar of money.

Dulnear continued, "Restraint is the warrior's friend. It gives him an edge against his enemy, making him difficult to read. It allows for surprise, and keeps the warrior levelheaded. And do you know what a warrior's greatest weapons are?"

Son leaned in, anticipating a revelation that would empower him against his enemies.

Then the man from the north said, "His mind, and his

legs. A sharp mind will defeat a sharp blade in any battle. Keep it focused; keep it growing and learning. Men lose fights not because they lack strength, but because they are dull-witted and stupid."

"Is that why you had me learn to read?" Son asked.

"That is correct," Dulnear answered.

"But why are legs so important?" the boy questioned.

"Because your first defense should always be to run," Dulnear said.

Son didn't like that answer. "But isn't that the cowardly thing to do?" he asked.

Dulnear said, "There are worse things than being called a coward. Besides, the opinion of man matters very little. Violence should only be used when there is no other choice. The man who is quick to fight will be quick to the grave."

"But what about the clash in the mess tent yesterday?" Son asked.

The large man paused, suppressed a smile, and answered, "There's a difference between a cheerful free-for-all and a violent struggle."

"I understand," Son said, though he really didn't.

"Good. Now close your eyes," the man from the north instructed.

Son closed his eyes, thinking how strange this lesson in defense was turning out to be.

Dulnear continued, "Now take a deep breath, smell the air, and imagine your surroundings. Are you at peace?"

Son was never really at peace, but at this moment, he did feel a sense of calm as he heeded the advice to be still. "Yes," he answered.

"Good, then stand up. Today, I will teach you how to punch," the man said.

As they both stood up, Son asked, "Aren't you going to teach me to use a sword?"

Dulnear answered, "Punch first. A weapon is an extension of your body. When the muscles are strong and skilled, the sword will be that much more powerful."

Over the next several hours, the man from the north taught Son how to stand properly when fighting, how to block an opponent's punch, and how to punch with power and precision. It was a long, exciting day for the boy, and for the first time in his life, he began to feel like the overwhelming sense of helplessness that had always hung over him was beginning to fade away.

It had been an exhilarating day that seemed to come to an end much too quickly for Son. The man from the north may not have had the cheeriest personality, but he never scolded or angrily criticized the boy. He was encouraging and patient, and had a way of causing Son to believe that he could defend himself and not be so helpless should he encounter any good-for-nothings that may wish to harm him.

For dinner, the two ate a rabbit that had wandered into their camp. Afterward, Son laid down, satisfied and tired. There was still a little bit of light in the sky when he closed his eyes and fell asleep, thinking about punching and blocking and overcoming anyone who would try to hurt him.

While Son was asleep, he dreamed that he was back at

the tavern where the man stole his money and he'd first met Dulnear. It was nighttime, and it was loud and crowded, much more so than when he was actually there. To his surprise, his father was sitting at the counter, laughing and drinking and having a merry time with the other men seated on his left and right. Son's heart was happy to see his father again, and he ran to the bar to tell him about his adventures and how he worked hard at the logging camp and was learning the ways of a warrior.

When the boy approached his father, the man turned his back on him and continued laughing and talking to the patron next to him. Son thought that maybe his father didn't see him, so he stepped to the other side and said, "Father, it's me!"

Son's father looked at him for a second and turned away without saying a word, and continued to talk to the man on his other side. This happened several times until Son felt a deep sense of rejection come over him, and he slowly walked away. As he did, he looked around the crowded tavern, and all of the faces were unfamiliar. He felt all alone.

Just before the boy reached the door, the horrible man who stole his money sprang out of the crowd and grabbed Son by the arm. Out of sheer terror, Son screamed, "No!"

"Scream all you want, kid, this time you're all mine!" the disgusting man yelled in Son's face.

From where they were, Son could see his father. He was still sitting at the bar, laughing it up with the other men. Son began to bawl as loudly as he could, "Father, help me! Help me, please!" For just a moment, his father looked his way, then turned away again as if he didn't recognize him.

Son's heart was now so heavy he could barely put up a fight as the evil man dragged him out of the tavern and threw him down on the ground. He kicked the boy mercilessly in the legs and side, then knelt on his arms, pinning him to the ground. "It's time to finish what I started!" the man exclaimed as he poured whiskey all over Son's face. Through burning eyes, Son looked around for someone to come to his rescue. He hoped to see Dulnear, his father, or anyone at all who cared, but no one came.

Then the man said, "Maybe next time you'll treat me with a little more respect!" and he inhaled deeply from his cigarette before releasing it over Son's face.

Son watched as the cigarette butt seemed to fall slowly towards his right cheek. As it touched his face, searing pain and light engulfed his head and shoulders. At that moment, he woke up from his sleep with a shout, covered in sweat, and shaking.

There was barely a hint of morning light in the eastern sky, but Son couldn't fall back asleep. He laid there, heavy-hearted, tears rolling from his eyes as he thought about his dream.

CHAPTER SEVEN

WRECKAGE

S ON GOT UP FROM THE ground when the sky was light enough for him to move about without stumbling over rocks or shrubbery. His knee was still a little stiff but was vastly improved from the way it felt a couple of nights ago. He gathered all of his things so that he was ready to go when Dulnear arose, and then walked to the southern edge of the clearing to try and see across the rolling woods.

The morning fog was dense, and it was difficult to see very far out. A mist hung over the ground like vaporous silk. All was quiet and peaceful until Son heard the heavy sound of hooves walking nearby. The boy stood as still as he could as he tried to gauge from which direction the sound was coming. He had almost given up when, stepping out of the mist just a few feet away were three large wise elk. They were walking and grazing on the dewy grass.

The wild animals stood tall and strong, with antlers reaching skyward. Son had never seen such majestic creatures before, and he stood frozen in admiration of them. Their gray coloring was the perfect camouflage in the misty hours of the morning and he stared, without ever looking away, watching their breath rise and evaporate in the cold morning air, desiring to savor the moment as much as possible.

Suddenly, all three wise elk looked up from their grazing and fixed their eyes on Son. His heart raced as their eyes met, and his awe of the creatures turned to fear as he hoped they did not see him as a threat. Then, as if frightened by a silent predator, the noble beasts darted back into the woods. Son's heart still beat quickly as he revered the strength and speed of the animals. He tried hard to see if he could catch a last glimpse of them.

The boy was still scanning the edge of the woods when he felt the ground beneath his feet shake. It took him off guard, and he looked around to see if his camp was being raided. The earth rumbled for a few more seconds, then he walked back to where Dulnear was laying to find that he was already up, things packed, and ready to go. "Did you feel that?" the boy asked.

"Indeed," the man from the north answered.

"What was it?" Son asked.

"Tremors," Dulnear replied. "The earth is uneasy this morning. We should tread carefully."

Son wasn't exactly sure what the man from the north meant by that, but wasn't in the mood for asking questions. The dream he'd had the night before and the poor night's sleep had him feeling eager to leave this campsite behind. The fog was beginning to lift and, since they were both ready to depart, the boy suggested they head back to the road.

When Son reached the road, the memories of his encounter with the man from the tavern invaded his mind. The feelings from last night's dream pressed against him as well. It was an unpleasant combination that made him feel heavy and tense. He found a long stick on the side of the road and used it as a walking stick, since he'd left his first one back at the logging camp. As he walked, he focused on the *rum pum pum* sound of the stick and his two feet rhythmically hitting the road. It was somehow soothing, and helped to take his mind off of the dream.

Dulnear appeared cautious as they traveled westward. Son wondered what was on the man's mind, but wasn't really in the mood to talk, so he just kept walking.

Before long, the road led them along another cliff ledge, but this time there was a steep crag along the north side of the road. From there, the two could see a long distance to the south, but could only see up the side of the crag to the north. As they moved along, Dulnear seemed to become more watchful with each step. Finally, Son decided to ask what was on his mind, but was interrupted by another tremor, much like the one he'd felt earlier in the morning.

Son braced himself and expected the shaking to stop in a few seconds, but it didn't. It continued stronger until the boy yelled to Dulnear, "What's happening?"

"Rockfall!" the man from the north yelled. He grabbed Son and began running back in the direction from which they'd come. First, smaller rocks were pouring down all around them, then larger rocks joined the bombardment. Dulnear ran with fury, holding onto Son while ducking and weaving to preserve their lives. As he was running, a boulder the size of a cottage fell just a few feet in front of them, completely blocking the road.

"We'll never clear the landslide!" Dulnear shouted. He ran to the rock face closest to where the large boulder had fallen and got as close to it as he could. There, he turned his back to the road, crouched down, holding Son, and used himself to shield the boy from the falling rock.

As rocks continued to fall all around them, Son could feel several of them strike Dulnear's back and shoulders. The large man kept remarkably still and silent while enduring the battering until a rock hit him on the head, just above his right ear. The man from the north released a low, painful moan while remaining frozen in his protective position over Son.

Even though the tremors had stopped, the rocks continued to fall. Son was shaking in fear, and wondered if he and his companion would survive this. He had never heard Dulnear make a sound in pain before and it frightened the boy even further. Then, at the height of his fears, when he thought he couldn't take any more, there was a last shower of gravel, and then stillness.

Dulnear remained as he was while Son shook in his arms. The man was in great pain and did not want to move too quickly, which was acceptable to the boy, because he felt as if he never wanted to leave the security of the powerful arms that were wrapped around him.

Eventually, the two uncoiled from the defensive arrangement they were in and began to look around.

"Are you all right?" Dulnear asked Son.

"I'm not harmed. Just a little shaken," Son replied. Then he noticed that the right side of the man's head was soaked with blood that was running down his neck and onto the shoulder of his coat. "You're bleeding!" Son alerted him.

"It's nothing to be concerned about," the man from the north replied. He then became weak in the knees and stumbled back until he caught himself on the rock face. "However, it might be a good idea if we sit for a moment to make sure we are fit to continue our journey." He then sat down and leaned back against the crag as his eyelids closed halfway over his weary eyes.

Concerned for Dulnear, Son took an old handkerchief from his bag and began to carefully clean the blood off the side of the man's face. His hands were trembling, and he wasn't sure if he was helping or not. He only knew that it grieved him greatly to see his devoted friend battered and bleeding.

As if sensing Son's concern, the man from the north said, "It's okay, boy. It looks worse than it is. A little rest and I'll be as good as new."

So Son sat down beside Dulnear and held his hand as the two of them stared off into the gray sky, listening to the wind blow over nearby trees, and pondering the gravity of what they had just gone through.

Son and Dulnear stood up and looked around. Most of the road was covered with boulders of various sizes, and travel meant stepping around them or moving them out of the way. Son led the way westward along the road, but it was slow going as he navigated through the maze of fallen rock by walking around, over, or squeezing between them. In pain, but mobile, the man from the north followed behind.

As they walked, Son kept an eye on the north side of the road and the steep crag that bordered it. He didn't want to be surprised by any falling rock that hadn't quite made it to the road yet. He was worried for his friend, but tried to keep an upbeat attitude so as not to give away how concerned he was.

They traveled like this for a full half an hour until they came across the wreckage of a horse-drawn carriage. It was turned on its side, with an enormous boulder crushing the two horses that pulled it, as well as the front half of the carriage. The body of the driver was lying lifeless a few feet away. The color drained from Son's face as he saw the dead man there, blood pooling around his body. He had never seen a dead body before and struggled to process the still, breathless form. Just then, Dulnear put his hand on Son's shoulder, saying, "Perhaps we can find something of use in the caravan," directing the boy's attention away from the fallen driver.

The two approached the carriage. There was blood running out from under the boulder, but the half of the carriage that was not crushed by the rock was fairly intact, albeit on its side. Dulnear pushed the carriage away from the boulder so that the two could get a better look, and scanned the interior for anything valuable.

The man from the north noticed a small handful of gold coins laying at the bottom of the caravan. He must have realized that they had been stored in the seat because he swung it open and watched four medium-sized canvas bags of gold fall to the ground, as well as loaves of bread wrapped in fabric and some formal women's clothing.

Both of their eyes grew large as Son asked, "Is that money?"

"Yes, it is," Dulnear answered. "Gold, and lots of it. There's enough here to live heartily for some time."

"Is it okay to take it?" Son inquired.

"I don't think the owners have much use for it anymore," the man from the north responded as he gestured toward the large boulder covering the other side of the carriage. He then took the bags of gold and put them in his satchel. He also handed Son a loaf of bread and took one for himself, which he immediately unwrapped, stuffing the cloth wrapping into his pocket, and started eating as they stood there looking over the carriage one last time.

Son broke his bread in two, wrapping half for later and eating the other half as he started westward again. They attentively walked through the muddle of rock and gravel for a while until they came to the place where the road was mostly clear and its elevation more closely matched that of the slope beside it. Relieved to be clear of any potential falling rock, Son quickened his pace just a bit, but not too much, because he didn't want Dulnear to strain himself after his injury.

Just as the two felt confident that they were in the clear, Son spotted a small figure sitting on the side of the road. It was a young girl that he guessed to be around eight or nine years old. She was thin, with fair skin, brown eyes, and long, wild, dark hair. She was dressed as a person of wealth, in an elegant woolen dress with lace embroidery along the front. She sat with her knees pulled high and her right arm wrapped around them. As Son and Dulnear drew closer to the girl, the boy noticed that she was massaging her left ear with her free hand and was making curious noises to herself.

"Pssssh, bang, ahhhh! Cshhh!" the girl went on as if she were in her own world.

Son got closer and stooped down on one knee so that they could be eye to eye. "Are you okay?" the boy asked with genuine concern.

"Great," the girl answered with a distant smile and a pleasant, singsongy voice, looking slightly away from the two strangers.

Not the answer Son was expecting. He looked up at Dulnear, hoping for a suggestion, but received none.

"Where are your parents?" the boy inquired.

The girl massaged her ear more aggressively now and a tear ran down her cheek. "Under the rock," she answered softly.

It was as Son suspected, but the answer still broke his heart. He felt the urge to cry with her but suppressed it. He asked her, "What is your name?"

She looked at the ground and answered, "Maren."

"Pleased to meet you," Son said cordially as he held out the remainder of the piece of bread he was eating. "Would you like some bread?"

"No thank you," the girl replied in kind.

"All right, just sit tight," Son told the girl. "I need to talk with my companion for a moment." He then stood up, turned toward Dulnear with a concerned expression, and said, "Her mother and father are dead. We need to care for her."

Bloody, disheveled, and sore, the man from the north looked at Son and answered, "WE do not need to do anything of the sort. If you desire to care for her, then she is YOUR burden." It was not the answer Son was expecting. He felt somewhat offended that the man would seem so indifferent about helping a lost orphan girl.

Feeling unprepared yet indignant by Dulnear's response, the boy raised his voice slightly and said, "Then I will care for her until we can return her to her family." He then stooped down again to see if he could get more information from her.

"Where are you coming from, Maren?" Son asked kindly.

"Ahmcathare," Maren answered.

The boy quickly looked back at Dulnear. Everyone in southern Aun knew of the great city of Ahmcathare, even Son. It was the port city to the east, where business and trade thrived. He looked back at the girl and asked, "What were you doing in Ahmcathare?"

"Father's business," was her only reply as she continued looking slightly away from Son. She never really did look either of them in the eyes. It was a trait that gave Son the nagging impulse to bob his head sideways to catch her gaze.

Son looked back at Dulnear again, saying, "Father's business. That must be what all the gold is from."

Rubbing his chin in thought, Dulnear answered simply, "Must be."

The boy turned to Maren again and asked, "Where do you live? Where can we take you?"

"Blackcloth," the girl answered.

Excited, Son exclaimed, "Blackcloth! That's where we're going! Would you like us to take you there?"

Maren simply nodded her head yes and Son extended his hand. She took it, and the boy helped her up to her feet.

"Are you okay with walking, Maren?" the boy asked as they began down the road.

"Yes," she answered shortly while looking back to where she was sitting.

Son then asked, "Do you have any belongings?"

"They're under the big rock," the girl answered, pointing eastward with one hand while massaging her ear with the other.

Son thought her behavior was strange, and wondered if the girl was acting this way because she was traumatized by the loss of her parents. He looked up at the man from the north and asked quietly, "Is she right in the mind?"

"She has the graymind," Dulnear answered. "She is divided in thought between her own made-up world and the real one. I have met others with the same."

Son remembered the illness his mother suffered in her mind. He wondered for a moment if perhaps she started the same way. This, however, was different. It was not an illness, for the girl had always been this way.

The man from the north, as if knowing what Son was thinking, continued, "She is fine. She's just a little... quirky, that's all." Then, as if he were not completely certain, he said, "Just keep an eye on her in case she becomes too distracted."

As the three of them walked westward together, Son's thoughts were conflicted. He worried about whether or not he would make a good guardian for Maren, but he also felt a sense of confidence, since he knew that he could work and earn money if he needed to, and he was becoming skilled at camping and caring for himself. It was a feeling of uncertainty and excitement at the same time, and he hoped that he could help the peculiar girl he'd found orphaned on the road.

Dulnear was impressed with Son. He tried to discourage the boy from taking in Maren, not because he wanted to abandon the girl, but because he wanted Son to count the cost. He wanted to test his sense of justice and compassion. He also thought to himself, *I don't want the boy to think I would take responsibility for her, if need be. This needs to be him.*

As the man from the north walked and thought, the pain from his injuries increased. His head throbbed to the point of causing occasional dizziness, and the bruises and scrapes he received seemed to grow in agony with each step.

CHAPTER EIGHT

SCARS

AFTER WALKING FOR AN HOUR or two, the terrain started to even out. The stony, craggy landscape began to give way to more rolling wilderness, with the occasional rocky outcropping here and there. The three remained quiet as they each processed the events of the day.

The road wound through a heavily wooded area and eventually crossed a creek over an old wooden bridge. "We should stop here for a moment," Dulnear suggested. "I would very much like to address my wounds." So they walked north of the bridge to the bank of the creek.

Son took several drinks from the cold running water while Maren sat nearby, sharing a story with herself. As the man from the north approached the water, he removed his bag, took off his coat with its clanging weapons underneath, and exposed his bare, scarred, and bruised arms and shoulders. He took off his sword belt, then reached into his coat pocket to retrieve the cloth that was used to wrap the loaf of bread he'd eaten earlier. He dipped the cloth in the stream, sat down at its shore, and carefully cleaned the blood from his face and neck. As he did, Son watched on, once again observing the many scars along the man's arms.

"I'm sorry for your injuries today," Son said with a sympathetic expression as he sat down beside Dulnear.

"They'll heal," the man from the north replied matter-of-factly.

"Do all of those scars hurt?" the boy asked.

"Only if they are reopened," the man answered. Then he continued, "A man does not develop wisdom, or strength, or the ability to endure, without acquiring a few scars."

"How did you get so many of them?" Son asked.

Dulnear began to speak, stopped himself, then took a deep breath and continued, "Where I am from, there is continual war. There is fighting over land, there's fighting over animals, there's fighting over even the slightest offense. Tribe fights tribe, and sometimes neighbor fights neighbor. Many don't even remember what they're fighting over."

Son continued to probe, "Have you been in many battles?"

"More than I can count," the man replied. "We are trained to fight from an early age. I entered my first battle when I was near your age. I found that I had a knack for fighting and led many successful raids."

"Were you considered a great warrior?" the boy asked.

Dulnear's shoulders slowly lowered and a sadness filled his eyes as he answered, "Yes, and I was very vain about it. But the problem with being praised as a great warrior is that warring men desire the glory of inflicting pain upon you. I lost both my father and my brother in battles with men who wanted to prove they were mightier than me."

"I'm so sorry to hear that," Son said sincerely as he began to think that perhaps being a warrior wasn't all he had imagined it to be.

The man from the north continued, "War leaves many orphans. It tears the soul out of a people. Something in the heart of man possesses him to keep trying to prove something. To prove that he's right, prove that he's better, prove that he will not let a single slight go unpunished. But in the wake of his aggrandizement is blood, brokenness, and bitterness. When I woke up to this truth, I tried to change, but it could not be done in the north. So I walked away from all I knew, and came south to make a new life. I had only been gone a few days before I met you."

"Maybe our meeting was meant to be," Son said with a sense of purpose.

"I believe it was," Dulnear replied.

"Do you believe that it was meant to be that we found Maren?" asked Son.

"I don't know," answered the man from the north. "But I'm not sure it is wise for you to keep her under your care."

"What makes you think I shouldn't help her?" Son asked with a slight hint of indignation.

Dulnear answered, matching the boy's tone, "You are too thin-skinned. Your oversensitivity can lead you into trouble. You are impulsive, acting without thinking first. You are lost in your own thoughts most of the time. How do you expect to care for someone with the graymind if you are scarcely present yourself?"

The man's words stung. Son felt wounded by his friend, yet when he thought about it, he could not claim any of the words to be untrue. The boy's eyes pooled with tears though he fought hard to hold them back. He replied with as much backbone as he could muster, "Be that as it may, she has no one else, and I will not abandon her."

The man from the north simply said, "Then you have much growing to do and little time to do it."

Son didn't say anything after that. He just sat there with Dulnear for a short while as the man cleaned and dressed his wounds. He then got up and sat with Maren. As he approached the girl, she lowered the volume of her voice but continued talking to herself. He let her keep going as she was, then finally interrupted, "Are you all right, Maren?"

"Uh-huh," she answered, with the slightest hint of a smile in her eyes.

"Are you sad for your parents?" Son asked caringly.

"A lot," Maren answered as she leaned her head against the boy's shoulder.

He wanted so badly to say something to help her feel better but really didn't have the words. He was just glad that he had a shoulder large enough for her to lean her head upon. Believing that maybe he was doing some good for the girl, Son realized that a person didn't need to be a warrior or a wise man to help another. He just needed to be willing. He then said to the girl, "I'm going to Blackcloth to find my mother, but to be honest, I don't know what to expect when I do. Her mind went ill when I was younger." He paused for a moment, then continued,

"My father went missing a while back. That's why I'm going to find my mother."

Not knowing what to say next, Son went silent as he stared down the bank at the flowing creek. As he did, he felt an awkward, pulsing squeeze just above his shoulders. He noticed that Maren was looking up at him compassionately while she reached behind him and gently squeezed his neck. It was a small act of tenderness and kindness that Son had never expected to experience from someone like Maren. He felt, at that moment, like maybe it really was meant to be that they had found each other.

After Dulnear was finished caring for his wounds, Son took a final drink from the stream while Maren stood nearby. The boy thought about their day for a moment and made a suggestion. He said, "It's been a hard day. I know we have some daylight remaining, but I recommend that we find a place to camp for the night."

The man from the north contributed, "There is plenty of tree coverage upstream a distance and the water is a benefit. Also, I believe we are near a village, and I would rather pass through it in the morning than during this time of day." Of course, the large man desired to rest his sore body more than anything, so he was in full agreement with Son.

So, the three of them walked north along the creek bank for a little while until they came to a small clearing at the top of the bank. The ground was level and nicely secluded, surrounded by tall pine trees. There wasn't much grass, and the ground they would be sleeping on was hard and covered in pine needles. None of them really minded, considering the day they'd had. It was just a relief to know they were going to be resting until the next day.

Taking advantage of the daylight, Son gathered some firewood while Dulnear began to make a fire using a handful of nearby tinder. Rather quickly, the two had a healthy fire burning to bring them light and heat when the sky turned dark.

The man from the north sat down to watch the flames dance along the logs the boy gathered, periodically nodding off to sleep and startling himself awake. However, Son took the opportunity that the remaining light provided to gather some sticks, a few smooth stones, and some twine. Then he sat down beside Maren to show her how he made things out of objects he found lying around. He carefully made a small catapult and proceeded to demonstrate how to launch pebbles from where they were sitting, all the way down to the running creek. It made the girl smile and Son let her keep it. The two took turns launching rocks until it became too dark to play anymore. There was something about the interaction that made the man from the north smile (when he wasn't nodding off, of course.) Perhaps it was seeing the children playing. Or maybe it was from watching Son care for another, in spite of the apprehension he showed. There was a hint of pride on his face, and he watched them until his eyelids became too heavy to stay open.

When the sky turned dark, Dulnear laid completely back on the ground, using a folded blanket from his bag as a pillow. Son decided it would be best to situate the girl between himself and the man from the north. He reckoned that she would feel safest if she was in the middle of the sleeping trio. Since she had nothing but the dress she was wearing, Son gave her his new blanket to use, explaining, "It's a saddle blanket, but it's very soft and warm. You can use it until we get you your own."

If Maren was grateful, she didn't express it. She just rested on her side and covered herself from head to toe with the blanket. From underneath, Son heard her say, "Good night."

Once he felt the girl was adequately situated, Son retrieved the old, worn-out blanket from his bag. It wasn't much, but he was glad he didn't get rid of it. He laid on the ground, facing Maren, and curled up as tightly as he could so that the insufficiently sized bedding would cover as much of himself as possible. With elbows and knees touching, he used one hand as a cushion between his head and the hard ground.

As he laid there in the dark, he could hear the sound of an owl hooting, the remains of the fire crackling, and the man from the north breathing heavily in his sleep, which was unusual, since he normally slept in silence. He could also hear the sound of a lively conversation coming from underneath Maren's blanket. He thought her habit of talking to herself was interesting and cute, and he smiled as he closed his eyes to go to sleep for the night.

Several minutes later, as Son was drifting off, he was alarmed when he heard Maren say loudly, "Hey!"

"Yes?" Son answered, concerned.

"I wasn't talking to you," the girl said from underneath the blanket.

"Oh, I see," Son replied, and he closed his eyes again, exhausted after an eventful day.

Not long later, Maren could be heard saying, "Pshhhh, ahhhh! Now it's your biscuit!"

Slightly agitated, but trying not to sound so, Son asked, "Are you okay, Maren?"

"Yes," is all she said, then continued her conversation with herself.

The boy tried his best to block out the sound of Maren's voice, but the later the evening turned, the more anxious he became to get a full night's sleep. Then, from under the borrowed blanket, Son heard Maren say, "How can I decide when you keep eating all the eggs?"

Trying his best to maintain a calm tone, Son politely asked, "Maren, would you mind being quiet? I would really like to sleep now."

"Okay," was her only response, and she continued her chat at a lower volume. Son was hoping for silence, but tolerated the quieter self-discussion until it gradually came back to full volume with a rowdy, "You wish I had a ham bone! Ha ha ha ha!"

Son exploded, "Maren! Would you please stop talking!!"

"Sorry," was all she said from under the blanket. This time she went silent, and remained so for the rest of the night.

Son felt bad for his outburst, and angry at being kept awake at the same time. He laid there conscious for quite some time, listening to the owl hoot, the man from the north breathe, and wondering if he really was ready to care for someone like Maren.

CHAPTER NINE

SLAVERS

SON WOKE IN THE MORNING to the smell of coffee. He peered over Maren, still covered completely by the blanket, and could see Dulnear sitting up with his book and hot beverage. The boy felt relieved to see the large man going about his normal routine. It meant that his injuries were not as severe as he was afraid they were. He cared about the man and was grateful for his companionship and protection along his journey.

Son crawled over to Maren and uncovered her face to see if she was ready to start her day, but when he did, he found she was still sound asleep. Gently nudging her shoulder, he said, "It's time to get ready, Maren."

Without opening her eyes, the girl yanked the blanket back over her head and forcefully commanded, "Quit it!"

Surprised, Son looked up at Dulnear to see if he had any support, but only found he had an amused smile before taking another sip of coffee.

He gave it another try and uncovered her face again, saying, "We have to get moving, Maren, if we're going to make it to Blackcloth."

"Okay," was all the girl said. Then she covered her head back up for a little more sleep.

Sensing that Son was getting slightly frustrated, the man from the north suggested, "Perhaps this would be a good time for some training."

Gladly, Son got to his feet and asked, "What will we be working on today?"

"Fetch a thin branch that is a little longer than half your height," the man said.

Son knew immediately that Dulnear was going to teach him swordplay, and he excitedly ran off to find the right-sized branch as quickly as possible. When he returned, the man from the north was on his feet, with a branch of his own in one hand, and his cup of coffee in the other. He was standing near the place where the flat ground dropped off to form the bank of the creek.

"Now," Dulnear began, "try to strike me with your stick."

Feeling conflicted by the request, Son replied, "Are you sure?"

Immediately, the man from the north whacked the boy modestly on the neck with his branch, saying, "You just died. A sword should never be drawn with a spirit of tentativeness. It is a weapon meant to kill or maim."

Finding the interaction entertaining, Maren uncovered her head, repositioned herself to a sitting position with the blanket around her shoulders, and watched intently while massaging her right ear.

Son explained, "I was just being careful because of your injuries from yesterday."

"We northerners heal fast. Don't worry about hurting

me, just try to hit me with your stick," Dulnear said as he took another sip of his coffee.

"All right," the boy said as he used one hand to swing his branch sideways at Dulnear's side.

The man from the north blocked Son's attack by simply shifting his own branch a little to the left, saying, "That's it? Keep trying until you've struck me."

So the boy swung again and again at the big man, getting a little more frustrated with each blocked or dodged attempt to land a strike. It seemed as if it was no challenge at all for Dulnear. He used his stick to effortlessly block, and took occasional sips of his coffee, often at the same time. Eventually, Son became so frustrated that he raised his stick over his head with both hands and charged at the man. Dulnear casually stepped out of the way, allowing the boy to tumble down the creek bank, almost rolling into the water.

From the bottom of the bank, Son could hear Maren laughing hysterically above. He felt embarrassed, but not horribly disappointed, since he was fighting against a great warrior, after all. Still laying on his back, he stared up to see Dulnear looking down at him. The warrior shouted, "Looks like you just died again! You'd better get up here so you can learn how to stay alive."

Son climbed back up the bank. His frustration had been drained out of him by the roll down the hill. He really wanted to understand this and asked, "What am I doing wrong?"

"Remember what I taught you about punching," Dulnear admonished. "Take a deep breath, be at peace, and make sure you have a solid stance from which to attack. The sword is an extension of your body, not just a piece of steel to flail about."

Calming himself with a deep breath, Son said, "Okay, I understand," and he took a solid fighting stance with the branch gripped in his right hand.

For the remainder of the morning, Dulnear taught Son the basics of swordplay. It gave Son a sense of pride and confidence to learn how to stand, block, and attack. He still had a long way to go, but it was a start. The two enjoyed the training time together, and Maren watched on with great attention.

Later in the morning, the three travelers walked for a short while and arrived at a village with many shops and a large pub in the square. There were surprisingly few people about and they were able to make their way through the streets with ease, and with very few awkward stares, despite being such an unusual-looking ensemble.

As they passed a large general store, Son decided he would like to go in and browse the merchant's wares. After all, he had more money in his possession than he'd ever had in his life, just from an afternoon's work with the woodsmen. Dulnear didn't seem interested in perusing the shelves of tools, clothing, and supplies so he stood outside near the entrance, scanning the village. The oversized, unkempt man from the north made the old shopkeeper a little uneasy and he kept his eye on him for any suspicious movement.

As the other two looked around, Son noticed that Maren was walking as if her feet were hurting her. He observed that she was wearing very formal shoes, with high heels and pointed toes. He asked, "Does it hurt to walk in those shoes?"

"Very much," she replied.

"Would you like me to see if they have a pair of boots that would fit you?" Son inquired.

Maren cheerfully nodded her head yes.

Thinking thriftily, the boy asked, "The shopkeeper may accept your shoes as trade for something else. Would you be willing to do that?"

Hesitant, Maren nodded her head yes again, but with less enthusiasm than a moment ago.

So the two looked for a solid pair of boots for the girl and found some that would do the job very well. They were tall and leather, with laces up the side. When she put them on, she smiled and began walking back and forth, talking in a strange accent as if she was imitating someone else she knew who wore similar boots. Son didn't quite know what to make of it, but he was happy that she was happy.

As Maren marched back and forth saying things like, "Ye be in for loads of adventure," and, "You're a hardy-looking lass!" Son looked down at his own shoes. They were old and shabby, with holes in them. He often had to tie fabric around them to keep the wind out and a little warmth in, and he thought about how he had never owned new shoes before, and how great it would be to walk the rest of the journey in a new pair of boots like Maren now had. So Son picked out a pair that would easily last him many years, as long as he didn't outgrow them first. They were a sturdy brown leather that slipped on and went almost up to his knees. To ensure that he didn't grow out of them too quickly, he chose a size slightly larger than his foot and stuffed fabric into the toes of the boots.

Son approached the shopkeeper to ask about trading Maren's old shoes for the new pair of boots. When he showed him the pointy footwear, the old man's eyebrows went up in an expression of interest. He looked at the boots Maren was wearing and asked, "Is that all you want?"

Son detected from the man's tone that the girl's shoes may have been more valuable than he initially thought. Thinking on his feet, he answered, "Not quite. I have a few other things I'd like to pick up as well."

Ambitiously, the boy went through the store and picked up a blanket, a long, black, hooded travel coat, and a bag for Maren. He didn't know what the girl would keep in the bag, but felt she should have one. When he placed the items on the counter, the shopkeeper inventoried them, and didn't look quite as excited about the trade as he did before. The man asked again, "Is this all you want?"

Not wanting to trade Maren's shoes for things for himself, Son asked the girl if she could think of anything else she wanted. "A canteen please," she said as she walked in a tight circle a few feet behind.

Son fetched a canteen off the shelf and placed it on the counter, saying, "This is everything. However, I would like to purchase these boots I'm wearing separately."

"As you wish," replied the shopkeeper, and he placed the canteen inside Maren's new bag and handed it to her. She put on her new coat, pulled the hood over her head, slung the bag over her shoulder, and went back to walking in a circle as she talked to herself about adventure and bravery.

Just as Son reached into his bag to retrieve his jar of money, he looked down and noticed how strange it looked to be wearing new boots with pants that were old, tattered, and too small. He asked the old man to wait for a moment, and he went back through the shelves to pick out new pants, a shirt, and a new coat.

He hid himself the best he could behind a shelf full of clothing, and quickly changed out of his old clothes and into the new ones. It was a strange feeling having a new outfit on. The shirt and pants were stiff and itchy, but Son felt like a rich man in them. Never in his life had he worn new clothing, and they made him feel grown-up. There was a mirror nearby so he walked over to it to see how he looked. For a moment, he just stared. The ragamuffin he had always known was replaced by a young man in new clothing. His hair was longer and his face and hands were still a little dirty, but he was different now. He was grateful, and wondered how things would be for him if he hadn't left the farm to take this journey. Son was jarred from his thoughts when the shopkeeper yelled out, "Are you okay back there?"

"Uh, yessir. Just need to find one more thing," the boy replied, and he grabbed a leather coin pouch as he headed back to the counter with his old clothes bunched up in his arms. Son then proudly purchased the items with the hard-earned money from his jar. When the shopkeeper asked if Son would like him to dispose of his old clothing for him, the boy happily handed them over, except the old coat. He had worn the garment for as long as he could remember and couldn't quite part with it, for sentimental reasons, so he rolled it up as tightly as possible and put it in his bag.

Son then transferred what money he had left to his new coin pouch. Then he put the pouch in the inside pocket of his new coat. His coat was dark gray and wool. It had a hood and went down almost to his knees. It was the warmest piece of clothing he had ever worn and he was rightfully proud of it. He offered the old jar to Maren and she accepted it gladly, placing it in her new bag, alongside the canteen. She also opted to fold her new blanket and stuff it in her bag, which looked a little funny because it caused the bag to look puffy and overstuffed.

After they were all done in the store, the two stepped outside to join Dulnear. When the man from the north saw them, he smiled and said, "Now don't you look like experienced travelers."

Maren said a quick, "Uh huh," and turned completely around to show off her new coat.

From there, the three companions walked to a nearby market to purchase some food for the next leg of their journey. Son had very little money left, after buying new clothes and boots, but he managed to get a little fruit and veg for himself and Maren to share. As they walked away from the market, Dulnear looked around as if he thought something was strange. "Do you notice anything?" he asked Son.

Son stopped, looked back at the market, then up the road, and said, "There aren't very many people here."

"A village this size should be bustling with people this time of day," the man from the north added.

"Maybe there's another special ceremony happening, like the one we encountered a while back," the boy suggested.

Dulnear wrinkled his forehead in thought, then said, "If that were the case, there would be some sort of festivities happening. It's strangely quiet."

They didn't speak any more about it as they walked out of the village to continue their journey west. Son was especially quiet as he enjoyed every step with his new boots. He felt as if he could travel forever now that he was protected from the elements. He even stroked the sleeves of his coat from time to time to admire the warm wool that kept the wind and cold away. It was a good feeling, a secure feeling, and a sense of thankfulness filled his heart.

The trio walked for a while along the road. Occasionally, Son would realize that Maren was far behind them. He could hear her talking to herself and, when her voice grew faint, he would stop walking and let her catch up. She would never walk beside Son though. At best, she would be a step or two behind, her hand on her ear, telling stories to herself. Sometimes this would annoy Son, but then he would remind himself that she didn't think like he did, and that he shouldn't take it personally.

After they walked for a couple of hours, Son noticed that they were gaining on a very slow-moving convoy of horse-pulled wagons. There were seven or eight of them, and each wagon was carrying a large cage. As they got close enough to overtake the wagons, the boy could see that the cages were full of people. They were well fed but dirty, weak, and sickly looking, wearing only filthy rags that barely covered those areas that should be covered.

Son couldn't believe what he was seeing. It deeply concerned him and he asked Dulnear, "What's going on here?"

"Slavers are taking them away. This explains why the village had so few people. They are all here in cages," explained the man from the north.

"But I thought capturing slaves was against the law," replied Son.

"It is," Dulnear answered. "These people go willingly. Do not even look at them."

Son didn't understand how anyone could ever go willingly into slavery. As Dulnear spoke, righteous anger rose up inside of the boy and he yelled, "We've got to do something!" He ran to the back of the last wagon, jumped onto it, and began cutting the rope that held the cage door shut. He was overzealous and overconfident, and didn't even stop to wonder why the cage was held shut by a simple rope with a square knot, instead of a chain and lock.

The man from the north ran after him yelling, "Don't, Son! Come down from there!"

Not listening, the boy cut through the rope and swung the enclosure's door open. As he did, the prisoners shrank back away from the entrance, huddling together at the opposite end. "What are you doing?" the boy shouted. "Go free!"

The captives said nothing, but all of the commotion caused the wagon's driver to take notice, and he let out a loud whistle to alert the other slavers. They, in turn, responded by bringing the entire convoy to an immediate halt.

When Son realized what was happening, he jumped off of the wagon in a futile attempt to avoid being seen by the driver. In no time at all, the three travelers were surrounded by a dozen angry slavers. They were well dressed but shifty-looking, reeking of cigarette smoke and scented musk. As they encircled the travelers, they pulled out knives and clubs. One of the slavers, the one driving the last wagon, stepped forward and said, "So you want to free the slaves, do ye? Well they came of their own will. And if ye want to start a fight, we'll be happy to give you one."

Son was scared. He remembered Dulnear's warning against impulsivity and was regretting his action. He thought about how his strong sense of right and wrong needed to be tempered with wisdom if he was going to avoid situations like this in the future; if he had a future, that is. He thought about what to say, but all he could manage was, "How can people go willingly with you?"

With agitation in his voice, the slaver answered with a curled lip, "Because they want what's easy," and he snickered as he glanced at his companions, who grinned their approval. He then stooped down to look down at Maren, who was nervously massaging her ear, and said, "Say, I know your type. You'd like to come with me, wouldn't you?"

Son was terrified. He was trying to process what the man was saying, but couldn't. All he knew was that his own actions had brought them into this situation, and now the one he promised to take care of was being harassed by this undesirable character. He began to tremble.

Just when Son thought something horrible was going to happen, the slaver stood up straight, signaled to the other men to return to their wagons, and said, "Stay away from my convoy... freedom fighter," laughing with a sinister cackle.

As the slavers began to drive on, Son looked at Dulnear, who was standing with his coat pulled back enough to expose the hilt of his sword, casually stroking the handle with his thumb. "I'm sorry," the boy said apologetically.

"You should be!" the man said angrily. "I told you to not even look at them!"

Seeing Dulnear's anger, Maren took several steps back and stood behind a tree. Son, still not comprehending what had just happened, pressed, "But why would anyone voluntarily become a slave? It doesn't make sense to me!"

Composed, but with lingering anger on his forehead, the man from the north explained, "Slavers go into towns and villages and throw feasts like you've never seen before. They last for weeks, and sometimes months. Rich foods, decadent desserts, and the finest entertainment are all catered. People from all over come because it's provided completely by the slavers at no charge."

Still struggling to understand, Son interrupted, "But why would anyone go to a feast thrown by slavers?"

"Because they don't know they are slavers," Dulnear answered. Then he continued, "They come back night after night until it's no longer special, but just a part of their lives. They become accustomed to feeding their stomachs, but they neglect their hearts."

"Neglect their hearts?" Son asked.

"There's nothing more important than our hearts, Son," the man from the north said. "Our hearts steer the course of our lives. If we don't care for them with meaningful things, meaningless recreation will choke them out like weeds in a garden."

Still foggy about the matter, but wanting to know more, Son just said, "I see."

"Eventually," Dulnear continued, "these people come to believe that life without constant feasting and amusement is just too hard and boring. But this is where the crafty slavers begin to make their move. They make them pay to continue enjoying the feasts, and pay they do. They give up money, possessions, family, even their dignity, and eventually their lives into slavery for the promise of more food, more revelry, and more entertainment. They become victims of their own sense of entitlement. They're not really even alive anymore, just entranced users blindly following the slavers."

This information grieved Son, and he still yearned to set them free. He asked, "But what can be done?"

Dulnear answered, "Some battles cannot be won, especially when the exploited do not want to be free. Say prayers for them, care for your heart, and refuse to ever become a slave yourself, by practicing contentment. If you practice contentment, then the slaver's lure will have no power over you. Perhaps your example will inspire the slaves to revolt against their self-imposed oppression."

With much to think about, Son and his companions began walking again. They didn't get very far over the next couple of hours because they wanted to keep plenty of distance between themselves and the slow-moving convoy.

Eventually, the road forked to the south and the slavers took it as the three journeyers continued west.

They didn't talk much as they walked through the afternoon. Even Maren was quiet, which made Son have to be more diligent than usual to make sure she didn't fall too far behind. The boy could tell that Dulnear was still angry, and felt it best to leave him alone until he showed evidence of warming up. Of course, that wasn't easy, since the man usually bore a stony disposition.

Eventually, they arrived at a place where the forest was thick on both sides of the road and they walked north through it to find a place to camp. They found a small clearing that was rocky but suitable for their needs and started to make a fire. Before it was even dark, Maren laid down using her blanket-stuffed bag as a pillow. She kept her hood over her head, pulled her arms into her coat, and curled up inside of it so all that could be seen of her was the tip of her nose.

As Son and the man from the north sat by the fire, Son apologized again. "Once again, I'm very sorry, Dulnear," he said genuinely.

Softening a bit, Dulnear replied, "It's all right, Son. I know what it's like to want to right all the wrongs, to change the world and rid it of injustice. Keep that passion, for it will serve you well. However, zeal without thought will only land you in trouble."

"I realize that more than ever now," the boy said.

Compassionate yet stern, the man from the north admonished, "I can appreciate that lessons learned the hard way sink in deep, but trust me when I say that it is far wiser just to listen."

Though embarrassed for his actions, Son was appreciative of Dulnear's advice. He made a promise to himself to trust wisdom when he heard it, instead of following his impulses.

Not long after, the two settled in on opposite sides of the fire. The boy took a while to fall asleep that night as he stayed awake thinking about what the man from the north said, and about the slaves, and how he wished he could set them free.

Dulnear sat up and gazed into the fire for a while. He was still agitated by Son's stunt with the slavers. However, the more he thought about it, the more he became aware of his own cynicism. It made him uncomfortable to think that he would believe someone was beyond hope. He felt contempt for the slaves and their self-imposed bondage, yet he knew that his contempt was not a good thing.

What will my legacy be? the man asked himself. *How will the boy see the world because of me?* They were questions that rested heavily on the man's shoulders.

Dulnear grabbed a nearby stick and poked at the fire for a while. He wished he could do the day over again, but he wasn't sure how he would do it differently. Eventually he laid down to sleep, as the burning embers of the dying fire glowed throughout the night.

CHAPTER TEN

BANDITS IN THE NIGHT

THE NEXT MORNING, SON AND Dulnear woke early to a quiet, gray sky. Maren was lying there awake, but uncharacteristically still and silent. Son walked over to her and said her name. "Maren?"

She moved in a startled fashion and asked, as if jolted from a dream, "What is it?"

"Nothing," Son answered. "Just making sure you're all right."

"I'm fine," she answered, and pulled her hood completely over her head so that her face couldn't be seen.

Son sat down on his blanket and tried to clear the morning fog from his mind as the man from the north enjoyed his morning ritual of coffee and reading. The boy worried that the man was still angry about what he'd done the day before, and was too nervous to ask him about training. Eventually, his fears were laid to rest when Dulnear asked, "Well, are you ready to learn some more?"

Son, relieved, responded, "Definitely! Would you like me to fetch a branch?"

"Not today, boy. I'd like you to use this," the man

answered, and positioned himself on one knee as he searched through the inside of his coat.

Son couldn't believe it. *He must be letting me use one of his swords!* he thought to himself as he approached the man from the north. Indeed, he was getting a sword for the boy to use. He unsheathed it and held it out for Son to take. However, it was nothing at all like Son imagined. It was just the right size for him, but it was old and dull and gray. It also had several nicks in the blade. The boy was both excited to finally get to hold a sword, but extremely unimpressed by the sorry thing at the same time. *Why would someone even keep a sword like that on themselves?* he thought. However, he thanked Dulnear, and did not give off any hint that he was disappointed.

The man from the north pulled out another sword from his coat. Son was expecting a beautiful, razor-sharp weapon, but it looked much like the one he held in his hands, just larger. "Now," Dulnear said. "Let's begin."

The two spent the morning picking up where they'd left off with the sticks. It was thrilling for Son, but Dulnear didn't always display the same level of enthusiasm. Several times he admonished the boy to cultivate a healthy respect for weapons, in order to prevent unnecessary injuries.

Eventually, the teaching moved from stances and grips to light sparring. The man from the north taught Son a handful of cuts, thrusts, and strikes, as well as blocks.

The two training together fascinated Maren and she sat up to take it all in. She winced every time their swords clanged together but seemed to thoroughly enjoy it anyway. She would repeat the patterns to herself as Dulnear taught them to Son, "Neck, knee, temple, foot, shin, up, down, up, down," and would often make her own clashing and clanging sounds when Son was asked to practice the moves with the air. If the man from the north was giving Son instruction and she couldn't hear it, she would just add her own dialogue to make it more interesting, "Hey, you stole my cabbage! No I didn't! Taste my steel! Pshhaaaa!!"

The morning went by quickly, and soon it was time to break camp and travel west again. This pattern continued for many days. They would walk until the sky grew dim, find a place to camp, train in the morning, and head back out on the road. Day after day, Son gained greater proficiency in fighting and swordplay. Maren enjoyed watching so much that she even started getting up at daybreak without any prompting.

One evening, Son, Maren, and Dulnear were sitting around the fire together after a dinner of squirrel and whatever veg they happened to have left between them. The man from the north seemed to be in an unusually lighthearted mood. Perhaps it was because they'd traveled for several days without incident, or maybe he was just growing more fond of his companions.

"One day," Dulnear began, "my father sent my younger brother and me out to do chores. We were only eight and eleven years old. We didn't always do what we were told, though, and on this day, we climbed into the tallest tree we could find. My brother was getting on my nerves and, as I looked at all of the leaves on the ground, I had an idea. I climbed down and made the largest pile of leaves I could."

The man's face became more expressive, and he stood up to act out what he was saying now. "Then I convinced him that, if he jumped into the pile of leaves, it would be like jumping onto a pillow and he would suffer no injury at all," he continued. "Without doubting, my brother stood on the branch he had been sitting on, jumped into the air with a, 'Wahooo!' and passed right through the leaves with a thud, yelling, 'My bottom, my bottom!'"

Son and Maren burst into laughter with the girl repeating the words, "Wahoo! My bottom, my bottom!" several times.

"Oh no! What happened next?" Son asked.

"Well, we weren't quite as secluded as I had hoped," Dulnear explained. "My father saw the whole thing. When he came out to see if my brother was all right, he whooped me a good one and made me do all of the lad's chores for a month." The man from the north then laughed heartily until he wiped a tear from the corner of his eye.

When Dulnear was done with his story and the chuckling had died down, Maren laid down just a few feet away in her usual position, pulled into her coat, with her bag pillow under her head. She could be heard saying, "Wahoo! Thud. My bottom, my bottom!" while giggling to herself over and over until she fell asleep.

Son and the man from the north sat together talking a little more about Dulnear's childhood until the man changed the subject by asking, "Son, I'm curious. What are you expecting to happen when you return to your mother? If she is as ill as you described, she may not even recognize you."

Feeling the joviality leave him, the boy answered

tentatively, "I'm not really sure. When my father never came back to the farm, I didn't know what to do. I just knew that I wanted to go home."

"Do you really feel like there is a home for you in Blackcloth?" Dulnear asked.

Son realized that this was the first time he had given any thought about what would happen when he returned to his mother. He knew that she was in no condition to care for him, and that their house was no longer available to them. "I don't know if there is a home for me anymore. I only know that I have to go and find out. Perhaps I will find a job and take care of her," he answered. Then he asked, "Can I ask what your plans are when our journey is over?"

Somewhat surprised by the question, Dulnear answered, "Oh, I suppose I'd like to find a place to settle. I left Tuas-Arum to find someplace peaceful that I can spend my days in. I think it would be nice to work the land and farm."

Son thought about his father's farm and how he so disliked working on it. However, after all he had been through, the quiet routine of hard work and self-sustenance sounded very appealing to him, especially if it included his friends. "That sounds very nice," he said. "Perhaps I could join you."

"You are very welcome to, Son," the man from the north answered, and he moved away from the fire to lay down, saying again, "You are very welcome to."

Son laid down also, thinking about what Dulnear had just said. He had never felt welcome anywhere, and it was good for his heart to hear those words. As he drifted off

113

to sleep, he imagined what it would be like to share a farm with Maren and the man from the north. There was friendship and laughter and sharing, and he dreamed that it was that way all through the night.

Dulnear also dreamt of living on a farm with his friends. It was a dream so vivid that the man thought it was real and he didn't know he was dreaming.

Each day he would rise early to greet the fields with gratitude and care. He found satisfaction in plowing and planting. And each night he would enjoy the farm's bounty with his friends as they shared meals, stories, and each other's burdens.

It was as if all of the anger, pain, and grief had melted away and his battle-weary hands had found peace in handling the soil and harvesting the fruits of his labor. He was happy, a feeling that had eluded him for most of his life in the north. He felt like he was home.

One day, as Dulnear was pushing a plow through one of his fields, a violent storm fell upon the farm. The skies grew dark, the rains fell in sheets, thunder and lightning shook the atmosphere, and the winds whipped through, uprooting trees and tossing debris through the air like dead leaves. He watched in horror as the gale turned into a cyclone and shredded his house and barn like paper. Something seemed askew to the battler, though. His uncanny sense for danger grew and eclipsed the false reality of his dream, and he could hear his own voice telling him to wake up.

The man from the north awoke and opened his eyes to

the black morning sky above. He could still hear the sound of thunder and wind in his head as the dream faded, and he felt heavy because the devastation he'd experienced in his dream felt so real.

Dulnear looked around the campsite to make sure Son and Maren were safe. As he became more awake and alert, he realized that something was very wrong.

The next morning, Son woke up early to Dulnear moving quickly to gather his things, preparing to move on. He had never seen the man in such haste before and asked, "What's happening? Aren't we going to train today?"

"No training today, Son. Bandits have been here, and I mean to track them down before they get too far," the man said with urgency.

"Bandits?" Son asked with surprise. "What did they take?" he asked, and took inventory of his things.

"They stole the gold and the two swords I've been using to teach you," Dulnear said.

Feeling incensed and confused at the same time, Son asked, "Why would anyone steal those two old swords? And how in the world could someone steal those things from you when they were hidden under your coat?"

"There is much I would like to explain to you, but we simply do not have the time. Get Maren up and let's depart while there's still a chance to catch up with them!" Dulnear exclaimed as he searched the ground for clues to the direction of the fleeing bandits.

With heavy persuasion, Son got Maren up and ready

to go. "Do you know which way they went?" he asked the man from the north.

"Their prints lead back towards the road. Perhaps they are headed in the same direction we are," Dulnear answered as he skillfully tracked the thieves.

Son had a difficult time grasping the situation. He thought to himself, *How can one so vigilant be robbed in his sleep? Is Dulnear having me on? Is he claiming the gold was stolen so that he can keep it for himself?* They were questions he pondered as he followed the man, moving speedily along.

When they were standing on the road, the man from the north looked around carefully, smelled the air, and said, "They are headed towards Blackcloth. That is fortunate for us, but we're going to have to move swiftly."

The three ran down the road as quickly as they could. Several times, Dulnear and Son had to stop to let Maren catch up with them. She didn't seem to be grasping the urgency of the moment or that shouts of: "Faster, Maren!" meant that they desired for her to run at a faster speed. Eventually, Dulnear scooped her up and put her on his back. The girl seemed uncertain about this and expressed herself with an occasional, "Woah," or, "Oh boy."

They ran through the morning. Even though Dulnear showed no signs of fatigue, Son felt as if his heart was going to burst out of his chest. He was sweaty and tired, but he was determined to be strong and keep up.

Gradually, the dense forest they had spent the last several days walking through began to thin out, and small clearings started to appear on both sides of the path. The man from the north slowed his pace to a brisk walk and

Son followed suit. The boy wondered if perhaps Dulnear had an inkling of where the robbers might be and asked, "Do you see something?"

"Not yet," Dulnear answered. "But bandits tend to hide in the woods, and we'll be reaching farmland by the end of the day. We have to tread carefully or risk alerting them to our pursuit."

Sure enough, within the hour, the three pursuers found a highwayman's camp, fairly well hidden, just off the north side of the road, set in a clearing within a dense cluster of trees. There were a handful of ill-bred-looking men sitting around a fire and three small tents encircling them. Dulnear saw them first and stopped to set Maren down. "We must be quiet so that I can observe the camp," he said. "I intend to assess the enemy." Then they silently approached a large stone just outside the camp.

"Are we going to fight them?" Son asked.

"I count only five men," the man from the north answered. "I can handle them on my own."

The boy was relieved by the answer but felt extremely nervous. Any doubts that he had about his friend's integrity were gone, replaced with concern for the safety of his company.

Dulnear leaned down and whispered, "I see several wooden chests piled together. That must be where they're keeping our things. Stay here, and I will retrieve them while the bandits are occupied around the fire." He then crept behind the camp without a sound toward the pile of boxes. The man stealthily searched through them but was frustrated to find that none of them contained the bags of gold or his swords. Giving up on staying hidden, he stepped out in front of the cache of stolen goods and greeted the men with his sword drawn. "I am looking for two old swords and four bags of gold. Where are they?" he asked boldly.

Startled, the men leapt to their feet, took out knives and clubs and faced the big man. They were afraid of him but ready to attack if the opportunity was right. One of them answered, "W-w-we didn't take them. I mean, they're not here."

Dulnear looked stern and threatening. He tightened his grip on the hilt of his sword and said, "I could never believe that a gaggle of inept fools like yourselves could ever steal something from me. It could only have been another man from the north like myself, but you were there. Where is he?"

"I don't know," the bandit replied nervously. "The northerner was with a man in a leather hat. He said that they were going to steal something, and hired us as backup in case something went wrong. We never touched any of your things, I swear it."

"Where did they say they were going?" Dulnear asked with a harsh look.

"Blackcloth," the man said. "The man in the hat was anxious to spend that gold."

The man from the north continued his questioning. "How long ago did they leave?"

But before the highwayman could answer, the sound of children screaming behind the large rock interrupted him. Two bandits returning to the camp came from behind Son and Maren and grabbed them. Dulnear turned to see what was happening, and it gave the other bandits the opportunity they were waiting for. One of them threw a long hunting knife at the large man and it stuck into his shoulder. With no sign of pain or hesitation, Dulnear used the flat side of his sword to knock the nearest man unconscious. From behind him, a man jumped onto his back and began pounding on his head with a club.

At the same time, the two returning bandits held on tightly to Son and Maren and began carrying them over to the others. Maren managed to extract herself from her captor and she grabbed a long branch from the ground. Amused by the girl's gumption, the bandit said, "Well, aren't you a brave one. What do you plan to do with that?"

Without hesitation, Maren yelled, "Neck, knee, temple, foot, shin!" as she whacked the man with speed and precision and he reeled backwards.

Surprised by the girl's actions, and emboldened at the same time, Son wrestled himself loose and also grabbed a sturdy stick from the ground. He remembered to do his best to stay calm and rely on the training he'd received. The boy's detainer wasn't so smug after seeing the way the girl handled herself and he held out a knife, ready to spar with him.

Heart pounding, Son continued to coach himself in his thoughts, *Be at peace. Do as you were trained.* And he did. His first move was to swing his improvised weapon around and bat the back of the man's knife-wielding hand as hard as he could. He landed a dead-on strike and the man howled in pain as he dropped the knife. Son couldn't believe how well that worked and he froze for a moment as he watched the man hold his hand up to his chest.

Furious, the bandit grabbed the branch out of Son's

hand and tossed it to the side. Before the boy could react, the man punched him just below his right eye, knocking him to the ground.

Son felt as if the forest was spinning, but knew he wouldn't survive if he didn't immediately strike back, so he sprang back to his feet and grabbed the bandit's injured hand, twisting it as hard as he could. The man howled again, cursing at Son. Without pausing, the boy added to his attack a forceful kick to the hooligan's groin. The man bent over in pain, giving Son precious seconds to retrieve the discarded branch. Using it, he pummeled him without restraint until he was lying face-first on the ground.

Meanwhile, as Son helped Maren defeat the other late-returning bandit, Dulnear peeled the man off of his back and threw him as hard as he could against a nearby attacker, sending them both tumbling into a tent. He then turned toward the fire and kicked a flaming log at the head of another would-be assailant, sending him reeling and screaming into the woods. As Dulnear approached the last bandit, the man began searching the inside of his coat in a panic. The man from the north sheathed his sword, leaned down, pulled the knife from his shoulder, and asked, "Looking for one of these?" The man just stood there, paralyzed, until the sledgehammer-like fist of Dulnear shattered his nose and knocked him out cold.

Remembering the children, the man from the north tucked the knife inside of his coat and ran back to the direction of their screams. When he reached them, their attackers were already subdued, and Maren was closely observing Son's rapidly developing black eye. "Are you okay?" he asked them.

"We're fine," Son replied. Then he enthusiastically said, "You should have seen Maren! She took a man down with a branch!"

"You did?" Dulnear asked Maren with surprise as he stooped down to her level. "How did you learn to do that?"

"I watched you," the girl replied, with a look that said the man should already know the answer.

"Well, I'll be. You are an observant one," the man from the north said with a smile and a look of interest. He then stood up and said, "I'm proud of you both. You were brave and fierce. But we must be moving westward before these highwaymen decide to have another go at us."

So the three of them headed back to the road and began traveling west again. Just as Dulnear had mentioned earlier, they exited the woods within a few hours. As they did, the landscape began to descend gradually into a wide, shallow valley. From where they were standing they could see, far off into the distance, the city of Blackcloth. It was still a couple of days walking distance away, but Son felt a nervous excitement build up in his stomach. He hadn't seen his home city in a very long time and he longed to be reunited with his mother. His pace quickened as he hiked into the valley with his friends close behind. Eventually, his view of the city was obscured by rolling farmland, but his spirit wasn't dampened as he repeatedly thought to himself, *I'm almost home.*

That evening, after Maren had laid down for the night, Son and Dulnear sat by the fire and talked about the events of the day. "Dulnear, why are those swords so important?" the boy asked.

"They are very special to me, Son," Dulnear answered. "They are my Cre-dreact, my heritage. My father used those swords to train me, and his father used them to train him, and so on, for many generations. They have been in my family for as long as anyone can remember. The man who stole them did so to disgrace my clan, not because they held material value. It is one of the ways men from the north challenge each other to fight, and why he didn't just kill me in my sleep. He intends to lure me into battle because of the great prestige that defeating me would bring. The gold was just a fortuitous discovery"

"How did he find you when you are so far from home?" Son asked with great interest.

"We men from the north are excellent trackers," the man explained. "We can hunt just about anything that breathes in almost any condition. According to what the highwayman told me, he must have crossed paths with that guttersnipe from the tavern. I can only assume that they plan to draw us into a confrontation."

Feeling fearful, the boy confessed, "I wish I had never run into that man. I should have just let him take my money and walked away."

"If it weren't him, it would have been a different bully," Dulnear responded. "We all must face our oppressors sometime or another. It is good that you learn how to do that now, while you're still young."

Finding little comfort in the man's words, Son lamented, "If only I never would have left my father's farm. At least there I was safe."

"True," Dulnear responded. "But your dream was to return to Blackcloth, and dreams are not accomplished by choosing the path of least resistance; nor are they typically safe."

"Well, now it looks like my dream may get me killed," Son stated with dread.

"These are evil men, Son," the man from the north asserted. "They stole what belonged to Maren's family, and mine. Evil men prevail when good people choose to avoid conflict."

The boy thought about his predicament. He desired with all of his heart that things were not as they were. However, he knew Dulnear was right. He chose to do the difficult thing by journeying home and by caring for Maren, and he had to at least try to recover her family's money. He also knew that if he didn't confront the man from the tavern, he would probably not see an end to the man's antagonism. "So, what do we do?" he asked the man from the north.

"They will probably be waiting for an opportunity to confront us in the city," Dulnear began. "A man from the north would want an audience for his victory. We will want to find them first so that we have the advantage of first strike."

"But how will we find them?" Son inquired.

"Like I said, we northerners are great trackers. Besides, that wastrel in the leather coif is probably anxious to have himself a grand time with all that gold. He'll be leaving a trail anyone could follow."

Son hated the thought of the man from the tavern spending Maren's money and hoped he could recover it before too much was spent. He was more nervous and scared than he'd ever been, but he decided that night, in his heart, that he would not let fear stop him. He would do it afraid.

CHAPTER ELEVEN

Bloodshed in Blackcloth

FOR THE NEXT FEW DAYS, Son, Maren, and Dulnear walked, camped, and trained as they moved closer to Blackcloth. Son was very anxious to arrive at his home city, but understood the value of taking the time to hone his fighting skills before trying to retrieve Maren's family money.

The boy often wondered if he should just turn back, avoid the confrontation, and let the man from the tavern keep the gold. It was a consistent struggle within him. After all, risking one's life over gold seemed downright facetious. He had to remind himself often that it wasn't just gold that he was fighting for, it was his freedom. It was the freedom to return home, freedom to choose his own path, freedom to care for others, and freedom to be someone who mattered and refused to be treated as something less. He prayed often to the Great Father during those days, understanding that what he was about to do required more strength than he had within himself.

Before long, the trio was at the edge of the city. It was a dirty place with dirty people who seemed to go to and fro without much enthusiasm. The sights, sounds, and smells of Blackcloth assaulted Son with memories and emotions both good and bad. It was a bit surreal for the boy to see sights so familiar yet foreign at the same time. "Much has changed," the boy said to his companions.

"Did you expect it to stay the same in your absence?" the man from the north asked, partly in jest. "Or perhaps it is you who has changed."

Son thought about that. When he'd left to go live with his father, he was a very different person; unsure, insecure, and lost in his own thoughts. He felt happy with the man he was becoming, and hoped that his mother would be too. "Now that we're here, what do we do?" he asked Dulnear.

"I think it would do us well to stop for a proper meal," the man replied. "My treat."

"Now that's an excellent idea," Son said.

Even Maren chimed in with an enthusiastic, "Yesss!"

The three of them walked through the main city street until they found a friendly enough looking pub. The smell of roast meat and bread floated out the door, and Son's mouth watered as he anticipated filling his stomach. They found a table easily enough, since it was still early afternoon, and the evening pub goers hadn't begun to filter in yet.

A round, rosy-cheeked barmaid brought them lamb, potatoes, and fresh bread, and they ate until they were satisfied. For a moment, amidst the food and friendly conversation, the feeling of dread that weighed heavily on Son was gone. He was blessed with a sense of contentment as he enjoyed the moment he was in, a very rare occurrence for the usually anxious boy.

The moment didn't last long, however, as Dulnear brought up the inevitable. "We need to talk about our meeting with the men who stole our things," he said. "It won't take long to find them, and it's important that we know what we're doing."

Suddenly, the heaviness that had been hanging over Son for the last few days returned. He asked, "What did you have in mind?"

The man from the north paused for a moment and said, "First of all, I want you to know that you don't have to do this."

Those words felt strange to Son. There was a sense of safety in them, but they seemed wrong. Still full of fear, the boy said, "Dulnear, you have saved my life more than once, and have taught me more about being a good man than anyone else. I would rather die fighting for the honor of a man like you than live knowing that I could have helped but didn't."

The man from the north closed his eyes for a moment as if Son's words felt like refreshing rain on the rugged giant's arid heart. "Thank you, Son," the man expressed. "You are a true friend. As far as a plan goes, we need to strike quickly. However, we won't know exactly how to do that until we discover their location. We will need to find it as fast as possible, since it won't be long before word gets around that another man from the north is in the city. I suggest that we find a place to lay low until tonight. By then, our parasitic barfly will be anxious to be out on the town to spend his ill-gotten gain. All we'll have to do is pick up his rancid scent and follow him back to his den of deadbeats."

"Okay, let's do it," Son said with mustered courage.

"Rancid scent," Maren added with a giggle.

That evening, as nighttime revelers walked the streets and filled the taverns, Son and Maren carefully scouted the lantern-lit city while Dulnear hid in a dark, narrow alley between two businesses that were closed for the night. The boy was fairly confident that he wouldn't immediately be recognized by his adversary. After all, he was wearing new clothes and traveling with a young girl, instead of a man from the north. Just to be sure, though, he wore his hood to cover his face the best he could. Maren did the same.

The two of them walked up and down the main street through Blackcloth's city center several times, peering in pub windows and looking out for a large man like Dulnear. He was just beginning to wonder if they were going to show that night when he heard an eruption of laughter down the street. When he looked, he saw the man in the leather hat walking in his direction. A sick feeling came over the boy as the man approached. He was traveling with an entourage of ne'er-do-wells, shiftless burnouts, and one man from the north. This man from the north was just as tall, if not more so, than Dulnear. He had long, dark hair that was combed back out of his face, and his beard was much longer than his friend's. He also wore a heavy fur vest, but made no effort to conceal his weapons the way Dulnear did. He carried a large sword like Dulnear, and several daggers hung from his sword belt.

Son kept walking in the opposite direction of the crowd and was relieved when they passed without recognition.

There was so much commotion and drunkenness happening that it was easy for the boy and his companion to change direction and follow without being noticed. They tailed the party to a large tavern at the top of the street and watched them all file in with very little courtesy to the other patrons or the barkeep.

The boy and Maren watched from the concealed doorway of a closed establishment across the street as the man in the leather coif flashed the gold around and tried to impress people by buying drinks for his lackeys and bragging about his northern friend's strength. It angered Son, and he was tempted to charge into the bar to take the gold back. He controlled himself though, and sent Maren back to fetch Dulnear.

She ran down the street quickly until she reached the alley where the man was hiding. He saw her first and was waiting. Dulnear asked, "Did you find them?"

"They're at the top of the street," Maren answered, and she grabbed his hand and led him to where Son was waiting.

The three of them huddled in the doorway together and observed the thieves and their retinue. Needing to know, Son asked about the tall warrior. "Do you know that man?"

"Yes, he is Tromdel," Dulnear answered. "He is a glory seeker and a braggart. It is no surprise that he would come this far to challenge me. He has slain many good men simply for his own aggrandizement."

A chill ran down Son's back as he considered the words of his friend. This was no good-natured brawler or warrior who kept his strength in check. This was a hulking murderer who valued no man's life but his own. He worried for Dulnear.

The three watched the night unfold from across the street until, finally, the two criminals and their followers came pouring out. Dulnear crouched down in the darkness as Son and Maren watched the crowd make their way down the street, toward the direction they originally came from. When they were a safe distance away, the big man stood up again and said, "Looks like your unpleasant friend from the tavern is using some of that gold to recruit a gang. It should make our job of following them much easier. Let's go, but be quiet."

Son, Maren, and Dulnear kept their distance and walked behind the group, being careful not to be spotted. Some of the party carried lanterns, and most of them were making a terrible racket. Even if the trio fell behind, it was easy enough to pick up their trail again. They continued to follow the group all the way out of the city and north, to a broad ravine where there was a large camp set up. It was secluded and wooded, ideal for a company that did not want to be disturbed.

"So this is where they're hiding out," Son said as the three of them crouched behind a large stone at the top of the ravine.

"A true den of flotsam, if ever there was one," Dulnear responded. He watched for a while, and noticed Tromdel enter and exit the same tent several times. He also noticed the man from the tavern do the same. "I think I know where our stolen belongings are being kept," he added.

"How are we going to get them back?" Son asked. "There must be thirty people down there."

"We will have to use our wits, my friend. They would like to draw us out in the city, but this would be the perfect place to confront them. If we surprise them, we will have the advantage of higher ground. I'm just not sure how we will be able to overtake so many people with just the three of us," Dulnear explained.

Son looked around. He noticed that the camp was confined to a fairly small area, since level ground was sparse at the base of the ravine. Also, most of the trees were toward the top and there was very little shelter down below. "I have an idea," the boy said. "We can build several trebuchets and station them around the top of the ravine. We'll bombard them with heavy stones. That should thin out their ranks."

Dulnear's eyes grew big with excitement as he replied, "That's brilliant, Son! Tomorrow we'll get to work. We'll station the hurlers along the top of the ravine as they sleep tomorrow night. The next morning, when they're tired and hungover, we'll rain agony on them."

Son felt relieved to have a plan, and somewhat honored to be the one who'd thought of it. He still felt very nervous and heavy though, as he contemplated the possible consequences of the choices he was making.

Later that night, they snuck around the camp along the top of the ravine. They traveled north of there to make a camp of their own. Once it was no longer possible for them to be seen by the enemy, Dulnear lit a torch to illuminate their way. They found a small, heavily wooded area where they wouldn't be spotted by nearby farmers and laid out their blankets, except for Maren, who still used hers as a pillow.

They didn't bother to make a fire since it was late and they wanted to keep their chances of being spotted low. Though Dulnear and the girl fell asleep quickly, Son was awake much of the night, deep in thought about his day. He was finally home, but not really. Things were familiar, but strange. He wished he could be with his mother at that moment, but he had an important task ahead of him first. He wished things were simpler, the way he remembered them as a young child.

The boy stared into the black night sky, hoping to see the stars again. He wanted to see or hear something that he could interpret as some mystical leading or encouragement, but nothing came. Only silence. He finally fell asleep, but not for very long. If felt like mere minutes of slumber before there was gray light in the sky above him, and the man from the north was moving about. He noticed that Maren was already up too, uncharacteristically. "Good morning, lad," Dulnear said as he tossed a couple of long logs on a pile.

"Good morning," Son said as he sluggishly rose to his feet.

"I paid a visit to the nearby farmer this morning and acquired enough rope and other materials to build eight good hurlers," the man from the north explained.

The man wanted eight trebuchets. Son was beginning to wonder if he should have spoken more realistically. He had only ever made one before and it was very small. These would need to be at least as tall as he was, and be able to throw a long distance. Despite his doubt and

132

reservation, he replied, "I'll start on the frames if you get these logs delimbed and cut to size. Maren, could you cut me several pieces of rope about this length?" He cut her a piece of rope to use as a guide before handing her his knife, which she happily took and went straight to work.

The three worked on the machines the entire morning and into the afternoon. When they were finished, the hurlers were just a little taller than Son at the frame. Dulnear was able to arm them with one hand, but Son and Maren had to hang onto the throwing arm together to lower it sufficiently. There was much trial and error as they worked hard to calibrate each trebuchet for maximum throwing distance. They tested them out in the farmer's field and, when each machine was adjusted to their satisfaction, they measured the throwing distance so that they would know where to place them around the ravine. It was hard work, and it was made harder by the nervousness that clung to Son like wet clothing.

By mid-afternoon, all of the trebuchets were ready for action and lined up along the south side of their small camp, just past the trees. Son and Maren were tired and quiet, and Son was considering eating a rabbit that had recently hopped past him. Just then, Dulnear came and sat down beside him, saying, "Son, I'm going to need to run off to get some things. Will you be all right here with Maren?"

The boy didn't feel very comfortable about that. He hadn't gone a day without the man from the north in months, and now he was going to be left alone, just a short walk from such horrible men. In spite of his feelings, Son looked at Dulnear with a confident expression and said, "Of course."

"Grand, but before I go, I need to do something," Dulnear said as he faced the boy and knelt on one knee. He looked very sober and it concerned Son. He continued, "Stand up, boy."

Son stood, facing the man from the north, uncertain of what he was going to do. He was worried that he was going to give him some terrible news. Maren stood just a small distance behind Dulnear, watching and massaging her ear. "What's going on?" the boy asked.

"It is time for your Tismatayed," Dulnear stated with a look of pride in his eyes.

"My Tismatayed?" the boy asked in disbelief.

"That's right, Son," Dulnear answered, and he placed his hand on the boy's shoulder. "You have become like one of my own, and I couldn't be more proud of the young man I see you becoming. You are like the *cairstos*, the rock-breaking plant that flourishes in cold, stony ground."

The words that the man from the north spoke rested like a warm blanket on Son's shoulders, and the boy stood as tall and proud as he could while tears rolled down his cheeks. He had never been spoken to like this, and it felt like healing balm on his bruised heart. "Thank you," he said humbly and sincerely as he looked Dulnear in the eyes.

"Son, I give you my name and my sword," Dulnear said, now with tears in his own eyes, and he withdrew from inside his coat the most beautiful sword Son had ever seen. It was a longsword, just the right length for the boy. It was polished and well cared for, and had intricately carved northern runes on the pommel and guard. "It's called Onaire," he said. "Blade of honor."

Still with tears in his eyes, Son took the sword, hands trembling, and knelt on one knee as well. "Thank you," he said again.

"Now, Son, I give you my name," Dulnear continued. "It means 'overcomer of great strength,' and that is what you are."

Son could hardly lift his head to look at the man from the north because he was trembling and weeping. Finally, he set the sword down beside himself, stood up, and embraced Dulnear with all of his might. The man returned his embrace and they both cried until they ran out of tears.

A third time, Son said, "Thank you." He felt honored and special, and all of the things that he wished he'd felt his whole life, but never did. As they sat back down and wiped tears from their eyes, the boy asked, "Is it okay if I still call you Dulnear?"

"Of course you can," the man answered.

"And if you don't mind," Son continued, "I was just beginning to grow fond of the name Son. Can I still be called that?"

"Absolutely," Dulnear answered, and he laughed a red-faced, swollen-eyed laugh as he patted the boy on the back.

Maren laughed too and sat down next to Son, nose pink from tears of her own.

"What do we do now?" Son asked the man from the north, still a little teary-eyed.

"I need to go alone to collect some things for our confrontation tomorrow," Dulnear answered. "It's important that you and Maren stay here to get some rest. It's going to take all of our effort to be victorious."

"Okay," Son responded, still nervous about being without his large friend.

Dulnear stood up and said, "Be at ease. I'll be back soon," and he handed Son a scabbard and belt for his new sword before heading northeast, out of their wooded camp area, and through tall grasses.

When the man from the north was out of sight, Son stood up and put on the sword belt under his coat. He looked the sword over carefully, examining the blade and hilt, speculating what the runes meant. He was still so shocked by Dulnear's act of favor that he didn't know what to think. He only knew how it made him feel, and he wouldn't trade it for anything.

He sheathed the sword and sat back down, this time leaning his back against a large tree. As he sat, he looked around the camp. It seemed strange to not have his friend there. Even though the man had only been gone a short time, it felt lonely.

Son noticed that Maren was pacing back and forth across the small clearing. As she did, she nervously massaged her ear. The boy had come to recognize when the girl was feeling anxious and he invited her to come and sit with him. "Are you nervous because Dulnear is gone?" he asked her as she sat beside him.

"Mmm hmm," she answered, nodding her head yes.

"It's okay, I'm here, and I won't let anything happen to you," Son said, hoping he could deliver on that statement if he needed to. "Would you like to hear a story?"

"Okay," Maren answered with a half-smile.

Son had never told a story to anyone in his life. He didn't even know any stories, so he did his best to make one up as he went along. He began, "Once there were three shining stars—"

"What are stars?" Maren interrupted.

"They're lights that appear in the night sky," the boy explained.

"That sounds amazing!" the girl responded with great interest.

"Well, the stars would come out every night," Son continued, "and they would watch the world below, fascinated by the trees and the land. One day, the three stars went to the Great Father and said, 'We're tired of just hanging in the sky at night. We want to fly over the treetops and get a closer look at the world below.' So the Great Father turned the three stars into elder eagles and they soared through the sky. As they did, they saw the animals and the people living their lives. They noticed how they loved and cared for each other, and they went again to the Great Father, saying, 'We're happy soaring above the land, but we want to know what it's like to live with others, to love and be loved.' So the Great Father tore off their wings and said, 'If you want to know love, you must know loss.' And he set them on the earth as three wise elk. Now they have many friends and are admired and loved, but they carry a sadness because they are no longer able to soar the skies." When he was done with his story, he looked at Maren for her approval.

The girl stared blankly at Son and said, "That wasn't a very good story. It started off nice with the stars, but the rest wasn't very good."

Son paused for a moment, expecting to be offended by her criticism, but instead found himself laughing. "You're wonderful," he said with a smile.

"Why?" the girl asked.

"Just because you are," Son answered, and the two of them just sat quietly for a while, eventually dozing off in the fading gray light of the late afternoon.

Son and Maren woke just before the last rays of pale afternoon light were gone. Dulnear had arrived, carrying two large burlap sacks. He set them on the ground and said, "I'm glad you were able to rest. We have a long night and morning ahead of us."

Still sleepy, Son asked, "What did you bring back with you?"

"One sack contains several clay pots, and the other flasks of oil," the man answered.

"What are we going to do with those?" the boy asked.

"Stones were a good idea, lad, but fire will scare away any of the gang that doesn't happen to get hit," Dulnear answered.

Son was taken aback by the man's plan. He struggled with the brutality of what they were about to do. He had never hurt anyone. And, even though he had become skilled at fighting, the appeal of being a warrior was at an all-time low. "Well, where do we start?" he asked the man from the north.

"We're going to head quietly over to the enemy's camp," Dulnear explained. "We will watch it from the northern edge of the ravine. Once the gang returns from their nightly trip to the city, we will come back here to retrieve the hurlers."

So, the three of them walked to the edge of their adversary's camp. It was difficult to do in the dark, but they managed, and they arrived just in time to see the group leaving for their nightly session of drinking and entertainment. They could see several men carrying lanterns, and the man in the leather hat leading the way, with Tromdel close behind him. It still made Son feel uneasy to see the man with the hat, even from such a distance, and it gave him a nervous stomach to think about what he was going to do the next morning.

Once the trio was certain the camp was empty, Dulnear repeated the details of their attack. His confidence in their plan seemed to be of little comfort to Son, and each passing hour only brought a greater uneasiness to the boy. The time passed with building trepidation as they waited for the party to return, and when it did, the clamor woke the boy from his horrific imaginations.

"They've returned," Dulnear said with focus and intensity. He took a ball of twine from his coat pocket and tied the end of it to some nearby foliage. "We may need this to find our way back once their torches go out," he explained. "Let's head to the camp and get the first trebuchet."

The three of them groped their way through the darkness and returned to their camp. Over the next few hours, they positioned the hurlers around the enemy's ravine. One by one they carried them, often stopping to gain their bearings in the black night. With each trebuchet, Son felt a greater sense of dread and a heavier sense of guilt.

When all of the machines were in place, there were four along the northern side and four along the southern side of the ravine. They loaded each one with a clay pot full of oil and set several oil-filled pots next to each hurler, ready to be set aflame before being thrown into the air.

They stood together on the southern side of the ravine and Dulnear began, "Son and Maren, when you see me light my torch, you will light yours and fire the hurlers on the northern side, setting the back of the camp ablaze. Once you have flung half of your pots, I will be launching mine from the south."

"What should we do once we've run out of pots?" Son asked.

The man from the north explained, "Son, you will make your way over to me. But Maren, I want you to find a place to hide. Do you understand?"

Maren looked as though she were not very happy with her instructions to hide, but she nodded in agreement anyway, saying, "Okay."

Dulnear then knelt on one knee so that he could get a good look at the children's faces and said, "Listen, always remember that a warrior's greatest weapons are his mind and his legs. If, by chance, I do not make it from this confrontation, get back to our camp as quickly as you can. I have left instructions for you there. Are we clear?"

"Yes, sir," Son and Maren responded. It was the first time Son had even considered that his friend may perish from his fight with Tromdel. It made him sad, and he wondered about his own chances for survival. He wanted to flee with all that was in his heart, but he determined to stay the course. Fatigued and trembling, the boy led Maren through the dark to the northern side of the ravine. They waited for the first light of the morning and for Dulnear to light his torch.

After an anxious wait, the blackness in the sky began to give way to a pale gray. Son could now faintly see the trebuchets lined along the top of the southern edge of the ravine, though he could not see his friend from the north. He waited to see a torch waving, but it did not appear.

Maren watched intently as she nervously massaged her ear and whispered, "Launch the hurlers, then go and hide," to herself repeatedly.

"You mustn't speak," Son instructed her. "Not even a whisper." The morning was getting lighter, and Son was worried that the sleepy camp below was going to begin stirring.

Just then, Dulnear stepped out from behind one of the trebuchets, lit his torch, and waved it in the air. Son saw it immediately and lit his own torch. All four of his hurlers were already set. He only needed to light the pots of oil and release the machines to rain fire on the camp below.

With hands shaking, he lit the first pot and moved to the next three, with Maren close behind, triggering the trebuchets as she went. Once the fourth pot was launched, they immediately started reloading the machines. The two of them would hang from the arm together until it was low enough to tie down, then Maren would place a pot of oil in the sling.

They had all four hurlers quickly reloaded when Son realized that he hadn't even looked into the ravine to see the damage yet. He stood at the edge and looked down to see that only one of the tents had caught fire and men were running out of it.

The boy quickly went to each machine and gave it a hard kick to the left or to the right to adjust its aim, and then he lit each of the pots on fire as Maren released the firing arms. This time, the pots did more damage, catching three more tents on fire and adding to the destruction of the first burning tent. It was beginning to grow more chaotic in the ravine as men were screaming, and others were looking to see where the attack was coming from. Fortunately, the trebuchets were set far enough back that they could not be seen from the bottom of the ravine, but Son knew he would probably be able to fire only one more round before they figured out where the attack was coming from.

The two youngsters set, loaded, and fired the trebuchets one last time, each burning pot causing more fire to consume the camp below. This time, some of the men below saw where the barrage was coming from and started to make their way up the northern side of the ravine.

"Run! Hide!" Son commanded Maren, and he began moving all of the leftover pots to the edge of the ravine. As the girl ran, he lit all of the containers aflame and kicked them over the edge, spilling a flow of fire down towards his pursuers, burning several of them. This drew the attention of even more men and they called for others to climb around the fire, up the north wall of the ravine.

Just as Son was beginning to panic, four fireballs flew through the air, crashing down on the hired thugs. Dulnear had begun to release his trebuchets from the southern side, drawing the gang's attention away from the boy. The warrior was able to reload and reset his machines with great speed, launching fireball after fireball into the rapidly burning camp.

As Dulnear was setting the last few standing tents on fire, Son started making his way along the eastern edge of the ravine to join his friend. It was difficult because men were fleeing from the fire and he had to be stealthy, often hiding briefly before making the next dash onward. Below, men were burning, and the sound of their screams terrified him. He found it hard to believe that he was doing the right thing by inflicting so much pain over a few bags of gold. He felt a sense of relief when he saw men escaping to the ridge of the ravine. He hoped they would be all right.

Son hid behind some shrubbery as he waited for another opportunity to run closer to his friend on the southern side. When the way looked clear, he decided to run for it, moving as fast as he could. He stopped again behind a large tree and reasoned that he would be able to make it to the southern ridge with one last rush.

As the boy scoped out the path he was going to take, a man came crawling out of the ravine behind him. Son was so focused on what was happening in front of him that he never bothered to look back. He was completely caught by surprise when he heard a man yelling, "It was you!!"

Son spun around. Standing before him was the man from the tavern.

"Tromdel said we would find you in Blackcloth, but I didn't expect you to try to burn me to death!" the man from the tavern shouted.

Son reminded himself over and over to be brave and not to freeze. As he unbuttoned his coat to gain access to his sword, he replied, "I figured it was the right thing to do after what you tried to do to me."

Red-faced and clearly angered by the brazenness of the boy's response, the man shouted, "Why, you audacious little brat! I'll teach you to make a fool out of me!"

"You don't need me to make a fool out of you, you're doing a good enough job on your own," Son retorted. He knew that if he could keep the man too angry to think clearly, it would give him an edge.

With eyes filled with animosity towards the boy, the man in the leather hat lunged at him. As he did, Son unsheathed his sword and swiped upward, cutting part of the man's ear off and knocking off his hat, revealing a pale head of thinning blonde hair.

Not expecting such a defense, the angry fellow grabbed his bleeding ear and took a step back. "Why did you do that?" he asked with a tone of surprise. He was clearly not a rationally thinking man.

Son couldn't believe the man was asking such a question. It was confusing to him. He answered, "Because you mean to kill me."

"I'm not going to kill you," the man answered. "I'm going to cut you into little pieces and roast you in that fire down there." He withdrew a long hunting knife from under his vest.

Once again, the boy reminded himself to be courageous, stay calm, and remember his training. The man swung his large knife at him several times, but Son dodged it skillfully.

Son kept blocking and dodging the man's attacks, but he realized that he would need to take the offense soon if the battle was going to go in his favor. As the man from the tavern lunged forward with his knife, Son stepped to the right and slashed downward at the man's forearm, cutting it nearly to the bone.

"Argh!" the man cried out as he dropped his knife. He recovered quickly, though, and landed a solid left hook on Son's right temple, knocking him off his feet. "You cut my arm!" he yelled as he bent down to recover the knife with his left hand.

Son got up as fast as he could and stood firm in a solid fighting stance. He refused to let the man's words confuse him or make him question his intention. He needed to end this or the fellow was going to finish what he'd started months ago outside the bar. Son attempted, once again, to disarm him, but he managed to block the boy's sword and kick him hard in the stomach, knocking the wind out of him.

Taking advantage of the boy's setback, the man from the tavern kicked him again, knocking him over and causing him to drop his sword.

Son felt like the world was spinning around him. He was frantically trying to fill his lungs with air and regain his senses. He could see that the man was almost upon him with his knife. He didn't have time to reach for his sword, so he rolled out of the way at the last second and got to his feet.

Snarling like a rabid dog, the man from the tavern slashed again and again toward Son until he had the boy backed up against the large tree that he had been hiding behind earlier. Aiming for Son's chest he lurched forward, but Son sidestepped and wrapped his right arm around the man's knife-wielding arm. As he did, he used his left hand to rake the man across the eyes. In agony, the man unintentionally dropped his knife, and it gave Son precious seconds to duck behind him, leap onto his back, wrap his right arm around his neck, and squeeze as hard as he could.

The man from the tavern spun back and forth to try to shake the boy off of him, but Son held on with a vise-like hold. Since the man's right arm was injured and bleeding freely, he only had his left hand to try to release himself from the chokehold, but it wasn't enough. Unable to breathe, the man fell to his knees. Within a few seconds he lost consciousness, laying face-first on the ground.

The boy didn't know what to do. He didn't want to have to fight the man again before he got away from the ravine, so he threw the unconscious man's knife in the fire, and kicked him in the head for good measure. Son ran over to get his sword back, then went to make the last dash to join his friend.

The man from the north continued to shower the enemy camp with fireballs. By now, there was so much smoke and fire that they were no longer concerned with where the attack was coming from, and most of the men had escaped out of the eastern side of the ravine, fleeing as quickly as they could. Dulnear kept an eye out for Tromdel and the man from the tavern, but the smoke was obscuring his vision. After he had launched his last burning pot of oil, he stood at the edge of the ravine and tried to see if he could make out the figure of his large adversary. Standing there, peering through the smoke, he heard a deep, gravelly voice behind him say, "Looking for these?"

Tromdel was standing behind Dulnear, holding up his family swords, goading the man into a fight. "I give you credit for the hurlers," he said. "You robbed me of my audience, but I'm still going to kill you and take your right hand back to Tuas-Arum with me." (Most men from the north were right-handed swordsmen, and it was common to keep the right hands of their slain opponents as trophies.)

An anger rose up inside Dulnear as he turned to face the instigator from the north. He'd traveled far and made great sacrifices to leave the violent way of life he once knew, and now it had followed him south, endangering those he cared for. He drew his large sword and said with authority, "Tromdel the blusterer, the only thing you'll be taking back to Tuas-Arum is the shame of defeat."

Looking Dulnear up and down, Tromdel said, "Brash words for a man who is about to die." He dropped the stolen swords to the ground as he withdrew his own large battle sword.

Dulnear stood as still as a statue for a moment. Part of him desired to clash with Tromdel and put the arrogant blowhard in his place, yet the other part of him, the man

147

who had grown wise to the cycle of violence, wanted to defuse the confrontation. He said, "This isn't necessary. Constant warring begets no good thing. Killing me would only put a bigger target on your back. It wouldn't be long before someone was stealing your swords and trying to kill you."

"That's a small price to pay to be the man who brought down the great Dulnear!" the man stated with a cocky expression.

Dulnear tried reasoning with Tromdel once more. "Just stop and contemplate, man! Death will come for you. You will not be able to walk the road without having to look over your shoulder for challengers. It will only make your life the poorer."

"I would rather die a great warrior than wander the southern lands hiding like a coward! You are a weakling!" Tromdel said with raised voice, irritated that Dulnear was stalling.

"It is not weakness to value peace!" Dulnear snapped back.

"Enough!" Tromdel shouted, and he brought his sword down hard toward the top of Dulnear's head.

Dulnear blocked the attack with such ease that one would have thought he knew it was coming before it was conceived. The two circled each other for a moment, then there was a fantastic eruption of blades clashing, kicks thrown, and fists hammered. It was brutal poetry, like a violently choreographed dance that was performed at magnificent speed.

As they fought among the trebuchets, Dulnear ducked behind one, causing it to come between the battling warriors. The two looked at each other for a moment with murder in their eyes.

"You'll never win this!" Tromdel threatened.

In response, Dulnear quickly thrust his sword through the frame of the trebuchet, stabbing Tromdel in the thigh. It was a sly move, but now that he was committed to the confrontation, he enjoyed putting the conceited ruffian in his place. "You talk too much," he said, and he tossed the machine aside like balsa wood to re-engage the man.

Now moving a little slower, and bleeding from his thigh, Tromdel seemed to be losing his confidence and fought more defensively. They sparred along the edge of the ravine, in front of the hurlers, back and forth, trading blows. Unexpectedly, Tromdel darted aside and grabbed Dulnear's large family sword from the ground. In a spinning motion, he managed to catch Dulnear's side with the tips of both swords. Dulnear made no indication of pain, but blood immediately started to trickle down.

"Put it down!" Dulnear demanded.

"No, I think I'll be keeping this. It will make a nice trophy next to your hand," Tromdel taunted.

"Put it down or I will kill you with it!" Dulnear demanded even louder.

"It's time for you to breathe your last!" the instigator shouted, and he spun both swords in a relentless onslaught.

Now Tromdel took the offensive, and it was becoming more and more difficult for Dulnear to block his attacks. Dulnear tried and tried to regain the upper hand, but just couldn't. Finally, his sword was knocked to the ground, and he stood there unarmed, waiting for death to come.

Tromdel sheathed his large sword, saying, "It's over,

Dulnear the Nawreek! To add to your shame, I will slay you with your family sword."

"Then do it!" Dulnear shouted. "I will not beg for my life."

At that moment, Son came running up behind Tromdel with sword drawn. The merciless braggart from the north caught sight of the boy out of the corner of his eye and let loose with an iron-fisted backhand that shattered Son's nose and sent him sailing backward into the fiery ravine.

"Noooo!" Dulnear yelled. He used the distraction caused by the boy to drop down and retrieve his sword. In one astonishingly fast motion, he picked up the weapon, slashed sideways, and cut both of Tromdel's legs off below the knee.

"Yearrrh!!" Tromdel cried out, and immediately dropped to his back as his lower legs came out from underneath him.

Dulnear sheathed his weapon, walked over to Tromdel, and wrenched the family sword out of his hand. "I told you we didn't have to do this," he said with a trace of pity. Then he plunged the sword deep into Tromdel's chest. As he did, he looked down at the runes on the handle of the blade, then at the mortal wound. A deep sense of regret and despair came over him and his eyes filled with tears.

Dulnear removed the sword from Tromdel's body and walked over to pick up the smaller one. As he did, he remembered. "Son!"

CHAPTER TWELVE
THE GREAT FATHER

S ON AWOKE LYING IN A plush bed of grass. For the
first time since he could remember, he didn't wake
up cold or stiff from the unforgiving ground. There
were birds singing in the distance, and he could faintly
hear a festive tune playing.

Still lying on his back, the boy opened his eyes to see
deep, blue afternoon skies. White wisps of clouds were
blown slowly and silently overhead by a warm breeze. It
was the most comfortable he had ever been, and he felt
that, if he closed his eyes again, he could sleep peacefully
for days. He stayed there for a little while, listening to the
breeze rustle the trees and the joyful waltz being played,
but he knew not from where.

When Son finally stood up, he realized he was on the
brow of a tall but gradually sloping hill. Behind him was
a wooded landscape, and in front of him was a beautiful
clearing, carpeted in the greenest grass he had ever seen,
running all the way to the base of the hill. He could see
a great distance from where he was standing, and as he
took in the sights and smells of his surroundings, he
could see great crowds of people gathering on both sides

of the clearing. Their numbers were many, and the throng extended from the top of the hill all the way down to the bottom.

The divided crowd continued to grow until they were much closer to Son on both sides. Normally, this would have made the boy anxious, but he felt no fear at all. The music that he had been hearing was growing louder, but no musicians could be seen. Just when Son was beginning to ponder the strange phenomenon, someone from the crowd yelled, "Son the rock breaker!" and the entire crowd shouted together, "Son the rock breaker!" and there was an eruption of applause and cheers for the boy.

Son was overwhelmed with a feeling he couldn't describe. The love and admiration he felt from the cheering crowd caused his legs to tremble, and he fell to his knees and wept. The acclamation grew louder and louder until suddenly, it stopped, and all the boy could hear was the beautiful melody. It was not a long melody, and it repeated over and over again, but it was the most lovely music he had ever heard.

When Son wiped the tears from his eyes, he could see the feet of a man standing directly in front of him. He looked up and there was a tall, muscular, white-haired man holding out his hand and looking at him with unrestrained love and tenderness. Son had never seen the man before, but there was something familiar about him nonetheless. It was the Great Father, and when Son looked into his eyes, peace and wholeness washed over him like warm ocean waves, saturating every part of his being. The homesickness he had felt his whole life was gone, and he knew, beyond knowing, with an unshakeable confidence, that he was finally home.

"Hello, Son," the Great Father said in a voice warm and comforting, and he helped the boy to his feet.

Son had no words. He just threw his arms around the man and clung to him, and cried and cried for what felt like hours, though there was no way to tell. The Great Father held the boy and stroked his hair, quietly humming the tune that Son had been hearing since he awoke.

Finally, Son asked, "Where is that music coming from?"

"It's coming from inside of you, Son," the Great Father answered as he lifted the boy's chin and looked lovingly at his face. "It's the song of your life, and it's beautiful. I am the composer, and you can hear the melody more clearly the closer you are to me. I would be honored if you would dance with me to it," and he held out his hands in invitation.

Son took his hands and said, "I would really like that, but I don't know how to dance."

"It's all right, just stand on my feet," the Great Father replied.

Son slowly stepped onto the Great Father's feet, and when he did, the music seemed to fill all of the boy's senses. He could hear the tune perfectly. He could smell and taste the music, and the grasses and trees seemed to sway to the melody. The Great Father and Son spun and danced and laughed together for a long time until Son became more aware that the song was rather short and that it was simply repeating itself.

"Why is the song so short?" Son asked as they stopped dancing.

The Great Father looked at Son with a tear in his eye and answered, "Because I'm not done writing your song, Son."

"You mean I can't stay here with you?" the boy asked.

"That's right, Son, but this sure has been a wonderful visit," the Great Father answered.

Son's shoulders fell and he looked down as he said, "But my life is so hard."

"I know it is," the Great Father answered compassionately. "But men do not become great on a bed of ease, and you are not the rock breaker because you've had an easy life. I have great things in store for you, Son, and your harsh circumstances are putting strength and compassion inside of you so that you'll be prepared."

For his whole life, Son had resented his situation. He had always felt unlucky and unfortunate, even after Dulnear told him that he was like the cairstos, the rock-breaking plant. But now he was able to see his life from a different perspective. It wasn't easy or pleasant, but he understood. He looked up at the Great Father with a fresh tear falling down his face, and said, "Thank you for my life." As he said those words, it felt as if the weight of a thousand burdens was lifted off of his shoulders.

"Oh, Son," the Great Father said with affection as he held the boy tight. "I am always with you, closer than a breath. Always remember that nothing matters more than my devotion to you. I love you."

After the Great Father spoke those words, he kissed Son on the forehead, and as he did, there was a brilliant light that enveloped the boy, and then there was silence.

———◆———

The calm quiet that Son experienced soon turned into an unpleasant ringing in his ears. The noise pulsated, louder and louder, to the rhythm of his slowly beating heart. For a moment, Son thought he was feeling the ringing, but then realized that his face was throbbing in excruciating pain. He let out a groan of discomfort, then he heard Maren's voice yell, "He's awake! He's awake!" as she ran into the other room.

Son could barely open his eyes, but as he did, he could make out that he was in an unfamiliar room lying in an unfamiliar bed. His clothes were folded neatly on top of a nearby bureau. As he struggled to figure out where he was, Dulnear came bounding into the room with Maren springing after him.

"Son! You're awake!" Dulnear shouted happily as he knelt on one knee next to his bed.

Maren stood on the other side of the bed, saying, "We've been waiting forever!"

"What happened?" Son asked through bruised, puffy lips. Both of his eyes were blackened and swollen. His nose was badly damaged, and looked very little like it did when he'd left his father's farm many months ago.

"You almost died," Dulnear explained. "In fact, I don't know how you survived. The blow you took from Tromdel would have slain a grown man, not to mention your fall into the ravine."

"The ravine was on fire. How did I make it out?" Son asked.

"It was Maren," Dulnear answered. "She ran into the

blaze and pulled you out. There were enough clear spaces at the base to get you to safety until I got down there to join her."

"And what about Tromdel?" Son asked.

The man from the north hesitated for a moment, then replied, "He has gone to join his ancestors," with a sorrowful look on his face.

"And the man from the tavern?" the boy continued to probe.

"I do not know," Dulnear answered honestly. Then, with a slight grin, he said, "But he was in such a hurry to escape the fire that he left these behind," and from inside of his bag he pulled out what was remaining of Maren's family's gold. There were three bags left, still a sizable amount.

"Did you get your swords back?" Son asked, though he was sure he already knew the answer.

"I did," Dulnear replied. "When you are healed enough, we can train you some more."

Son wasn't sure he wanted any more training. Fighting felt very distasteful to him after their confrontation at the ravine. He asked, "Where are we?"

"We are at the house of the farmer who provided us materials for our trebuchets," Dulnear answered. "It turns out that he owns the land that we camped on, and the ravine that those scoundrels were occupying. In fact, he owns most of the land around here. He was very grateful that we ran those undesirables off, so he opened up his home to us. When you're feeling better, I'll introduce you to him."

"Thank him for me," Son said, feeling like he was going to drift back to sleep.

Just then, Maren chimed in, "I made you something." She produced a stuffed animal that she had sewn together out of scraps of fabric and bits of cotton and straw.

The boy took the stuffed animal and tried his best to look grateful through his black and purple swollen face. He said, "Thank you. What is it?"

"It's a wise elk," Maren answered. "I made one for each of us."

Son remembered the story he had told the girl and began to chuckle, but as he did, incredible pain surged through his face, and his body tightened in response.

"Be careful there, Son," Dulnear reacted. "It's going to take a while to heal. I tried my best to set your nose, but I'm afraid I couldn't return it to its original boyish form." Trying to sound optimistic, he continued, "Now you look rugged and confident."

Son tried to imagine what he looked like. He hadn't seen a mirror since he'd bought his new clothes. Before that, he had only seen one a handful of times in his life. He concluded that it would be best if he just didn't think about it for a while.

The three of them visited some more, retelling what happened at the ravine from their unique perspectives. It wasn't long though before Son drifted off to sleep in the middle of the conversation. He was still badly injured and needed his rest.

As the weeks went by and Son regained his strength, he became acquainted with the old farmer who took him and his companions in. His name was Aesef. He was short and round but muscular, with unkempt gray hair and a long, gray beard. Although he was rich in property, and quite wealthy, he still dressed like a simple farmer, and his hands had the look of someone who had spent most of his life working the land. Daily he would walk the fields, puffing at his pipe and checking with the laborers. He was very kind to them and appreciated their hard work.

When Son felt up to it, he would walk with Aesef. They got to know each other quite well, and the man seemed particularly interested in the stories Son told about life in Blackcloth before he went to live with his father. He had spent his entire life living outside of the city, but almost never ventured into it.

The gracious farmer became quite fond of the boy over time, and one day, he asked, "Son, what is your plan once you reunite with your mother?"

Son paused for a moment. Dulnear had asked him the same question back on the road, but he didn't have a confident answer. He said, "I don't know. I want to release her from the sanitarium and live with her again."

"Taking care of someone with an illness like your mother's can be quite taxing," Aesef replied. "How will you support the two of you?"

Son had never thought about how he would care for his mother and earn a living at the same time. He knew she would need quite a bit of attention, and didn't know how he would provide it. "I really don't know," he answered.

"I have an idea," the old farmer said. "If you would like, you can come work for me on the farm. I pay an honest wage."

Son felt honored that the man would offer him

employment. He respected the farmer, and noticed how well he treated his workers. "Thank you for the offer, Aesef," he replied. "But I don't think laborer's quarters would be the appropriate place to care for my mother."

"Of course," Aesef responded. "That's why you and your mother would live with me in my house. My servants can care for your mother while you work the farm."

Son was touched deeply by the generosity of the old man. He wondered what Aesef saw in him that would cause him to make such an offer. The man's house was very large. In fact, he had never been in a house so big. He imagined that he and his mother would be quite happy there. It didn't take long for him to make his decision. He said, "Thank you. I would like that very much," with a tired smile on his face.

"My door is always open to you, Son," the farmer said. "After you've settled your affairs in Blackcloth, feel free to come back whenever you're ready."

"Thank you," Son repeated, and the two continued walking together until it was time to go back to the house for dinner.

As Son continued to recover from his injuries, he would walk the farm more and more. Sometimes he walked with Aesef, but most of the time it was alone. He used the time to contemplate the events in his life since he'd left his father's farm. He especially thought about the Tismatayed with Dulnear, meeting the Great Father, and the kindness of the old farmer. He felt stronger now, less anxious, and more at peace with himself. He was indeed a different boy now, and that suited him fine.

One morning, when Son was almost completely healed and ready to be reunited with his mother, he walked the fields one last time. He thought about Aesef's offer, and felt very content with the thought of living there with the old farmer. He felt like the farm was a healing place for him in more ways than one.

As he walked alone, he found himself wandering as far out as the camp where they'd built the trebuchets, and the ravine where he almost lost his life. All of the trees were black and twisted from the fire, and it seemed eerily destitute. The hurlers stood along the edge of the ravine like silent memorials to a powerful turning point in his life. It felt very lonely for Son to be there without Dulnear and Maren.

He stood at the edge of the ravine, listening to the breeze, and recalling his fight with the man from the tavern. It brought him sadness to think about the cruelties of life, and he wished that people cared more for peace than they did about how they were perceived by others. It was pride that brought the man from the tavern and Tromdel to defeat, and Son paused to say a quick prayer to the Great Father for the humility needed to walk in peace.

When he was finished reflecting, Son walked back to the house. When he arrived there, he found Dulnear and Maren with their things gathered and ready to go. Aesef had an early afternoon lunch prepared for them, and the four of them enjoyed one last meal and rousing conversation together. They talked about their weeks spent there in the hospitality of the old farmer, and they expressed their gratitude profusely for his care and generosity. When they were done, they said their good-byes.

Son felt privileged to have made a friend like Aesef, and he thanked him again for his kindhearted offer. "I hope to see you soon," the boy expressed as the trio made their way out the door.

"And I hope to see you, Son," Aesef replied, adding, "and your mother!"

The boy smiled and hugged the old man, as did Maren and Dulnear. Even though they'd only known the farmer for a few weeks, he felt like family to them. Each of them would have preferred to stay in his company longer, but the purpose for Son's journey was still ahead.

CHAPTER THIRTEEN
Homecoming

T HE THREE TRAVELERS WALKED BACK towards Blackcloth. As they passed the burned-out ravine, they said very little to each other. Even though Son had already spent time reflecting there, it still felt strange to him, and it stirred up emotions he would rather not feel.

Once they were near the city limits, Dulnear asked Son, "Well, boy, what is your plan?"

Son stopped walking for a moment and the others followed suit, facing him. "I think we should take Maren home first," he answered. Then he asked the girl, "Is that all right with you?"

"Okay," she answered, but the look on her face said she was sad to be leaving her companions.

"It'll be all right," Son tried to assure her. "We'll be living close enough to each other to visit as often as we want."

Son's statement did little to comfort the girl, and she just nodded her head in acknowledgement.

The boy took Maren's hand and asked, "Can you show us where your house is?"

"Uh-huh," she answered, and she led them through the narrow stone streets to a high section on the southern edge of the city. It was full of impressive homes that overlooked the lower sections to the north and the southern countryside. When they arrived at her house, she said, "Here it is."

It was a very nice home, but not the sprawling estate Son was expecting. It had four bedrooms and a larger than average garden that was overgrown and neglected. The boy thought it was unusual that people of such means would allow their property to look so shabby. They opened the gate and walked up to the door together.

It looked as if no one was home but Son knocked anyway. There was no answer. Son knocked several more times, but each time there was only silence in return. Just then, it dawned on him that perhaps Maren didn't have any other family. He asked her, "Do you not have any brothers or sisters?"

"No," she answered plainly.

"Aunts and uncles?" he continued to probe.

"I don't have any," she replied.

"Servants?" the boy asked, as the full weight of Maren's loss started to become much clearer to him.

"My father dismissed them before we left for Ahm-cathare," the girl answered.

Son paused for a moment. Even though he cared for Maren deeply, his expectation was to return her home before reuniting with his mother. He took a minute to mentally adjust his plans as he remembered what it was like to try to care for himself on his father's farm. He stooped down a little so that he could be eye to eye with the girl and asked, "Maren, would you like to stay with me?" He didn't know how he would take care of her, especially if he was caring for his mother. He just knew that she had no one else and that it was the right thing to do.

Maren smiled a sad smile and nodded her head yes.

Son gave her a warm hug and assured her that everything was going to be all right, then he asked her, "Is there anything you would like to get from your house?"

"Yes," she answered, "but I don't have a key."

Son looked at Dulnear and asked, with a facial expression, if he could get them into the house. The man from the north stepped forward with a dagger and forced it into the lock. When he turned it, the sound of breaking metal could be heard and the door came open for them.

When they stepped inside, Maren slowly walked into the large front room and looked around. She smelled the air and said, "It smells like Mother and Father," and her bottom lip quivered as tears fell from her eyes.

Son was surprised to see her so emotional, especially since she hardly seemed sad immediately after her parents had died. Perhaps it took a while to process her loss, or maybe it was the graymind. Regardless of the reason, his heart broke to see her in tears, and he gave her another hug and let her cry on his shoulder for as long as she needed.

When Maren was composed, she walked slowly through the house, taking in the sights and smells of her home one last time. When she reached her room, she opened a chest and pulled out a small stack of letters. They were notes her parents had written to her on each of her birthdays. She put them in her bag, along with a handmade sketchpad, some pencils, and a few underthings.

When she came back to the front room to rejoin her friends, she said with a smile, "I got my sketchbook."

"You draw?" Son asked.

"Uh-huh," she answered enthusiastically. "Would you like to see my drawings?"

The boy was anxious to move on to the sanitarium, but was still moved by compassion for Maren, so he said, "Of course we do!" The three of them sat down together in the large room as the girl proudly displayed her sketches to them.

Son and Dulnear were pleasantly surprised by the skill Maren possessed. They complimented each one with enthusiasm, and the sadness disappeared from the girl's face as she gave detailed accounts of what each drawing was, what the story was behind the picture, and what inspired her to draw it.

When they were done, Son said, "Well, I think we should walk to the sanitarium before it gets too late," and the other two agreed. Knowing that, after all he had been through, he was finally going to be reunited with his mother, the boy's stomach filled with butterflies and a nervous excitement came over him.

As they left the house and headed down the street, Son thought about all of the different ways his reunion could go. He mentally practiced his greeting and how he would explain to her why he was there. Above all, though, he hoped more than anything that she was somehow better, that he could reach her, and that she would know who he was and love him as she used to.

The three approached the sanitarium on the western edge of the city. It was a large building, old but well cared for, and it sat on a large parcel of land surrounded by shabby houses and dirty streets. When they walked onto the property, a flood of emotions came over Son. He remembered saying good-bye to his mother there, three seasons ago, and boarding a carriage to go live with his father. He felt a discomfort in his chest as he recalled the events, and as he looked around, it was like peering back in time to the most painful moment in his life.

They stepped inside the building, and the haunting sounds of the insane could be heard echoing through the halls. It reeked of human waste and sweat, and it made Maren very anxious. She nervously massaged her ear and began whispering something to herself as they sought someone out who could lead them to Son's mother.

It wasn't long before they found a friar who was able to assist them. He was a kind man who seemed eager to help, and had a surprisingly upbeat disposition, despite working in such a cheerless environment. When Son explained who he was and why they were there, the man asked them to stay put while he went to find the location of Son's mother.

As they waited for what seemed like a very long time, Dulnear attempted to alleviate the tension they all felt by quipping, "So, how would you like to work here?" and he smiled an awkward grin to let them know he was trying to bring a little levity.

It didn't work. "I wouldn't," Son responded, and they all went back to waiting silently.

Finally, the kind friar returned. He looked at Son and said, "I think we should sit down together."

Those words didn't sit well with Son. Hooks of dread sank deep into the boy's shoulders, and he tried his best to still his shaking hands as he followed the friar outside to a table and chairs that were situated in the garden.

When they were all seated, Son asked, "Where is my mother?"

"I spoke with Brother Messocht," the friar began. "He was one of the friars who cared for your mother. As you know, her condition was quite severe when she arrived. She spent most days sitting by the window in her room, looking outside, unable to communicate with anyone. As time went by, she grew worse. It was as if she forgot how to walk, how to find her chair, or even how to eat and drink. The brothers tried to give her food every day, but they couldn't get her to swallow. About a year ago, she passed away."

Son felt dizzy and heavy, and wondered for a moment if he was possibly dreaming. His heart felt as if a large piece of it was torn out. The thought that he would never see his mother again was a weight too heavy to bear. However, he maintained his composure on the outside and asked, "May I collect her things?"

"Her things have already been collected," the friar answered. "But if there's anything else that I can do for you, please let me know. I'm very sorry for your loss."

"Thank you," Son answered sadly.

The four of them stood up from the table together. As the friar walked away, questions began swirling through Son's mind. He wondered if his mother had suffered. He wondered if the friars were truly diligent in their care for her. And he wondered who it was that came for her belongings. Ever since he'd left his father's farm, his sole purpose was to return to his mother, and now that purpose was taken away.

Dulnear placed his hand on the boy's shoulder and said, "I'm so sorry, Son. This must be incredibly painful."

"It is," the boy answered. "I feel robbed. It's not fair!" He began to cry as the man from the north embraced him.

After Son sobbed for a while, Dulnear asked him gently, "What would you like to do?"

The boy thought for a minute and said, "I would like to pay a visit to my uncle," as he wiped the tears from his eyes and composed himself. He was hoping his uncle had his mother's belongings, and that maybe he would let him keep something as a memento.

"Okay," the large man replied. "You lead the way."

So Son led the three of them away from the sanitarium and through the streets to his uncle's house.

As they walked up to Uncle Kione's house, Son noticed that it wasn't as nice and well-kept as he remembered it to be. It was just south of the city's center, in a row of attached homes. The surrounding homes were fairly well-kept, which made his uncle's look run-down in comparison. He nervously approached the door and knocked. Almost immediately, he heard his uncle's voice yell from inside, "Come in!"

Son had a nervous feeling in his stomach as he opened the door. He had never known his uncle to be a very kind man, and wasn't expecting a warm welcome. His friends waited outside while he went in.

"Hello, Uncle," the boy began to say, but went speechless when he looked into the house. The front door opened into a room with a desk on the left, and a small setting of chairs with a tea table on the right. Beyond this room was a kitchen. To the far left was a staircase that led up to his uncle's bedroom. The inside of the house was in worse condition than the outside. Dirty dishes and assorted garbage littered the kitchen and front room. His uncle was seated at the desk, but sitting in one of the chairs to the right was Son's father.

Son couldn't believe it. All this time he'd wondered what had happened to his father, and here he was. Before he had a chance to say anything, Uncle Kione asked, "Son, what are you doing here?" in an irritated tone.

Son didn't bother to answer right away. He was looking intently at his father. He looked different somehow. He seemed smaller, and not as intimidating. He had clearly been drinking heavily, and looked as if he hadn't bathed or changed his clothes in quite some time. He didn't look directly at Son, but repeated Kione's question, "What are you doing here?"

The boy was taken aback because it had been so long since either of these men had seen him, yet there was no welcome and no acknowledgement that his nose looked different. "I came back," was all that Son could say.

"So you just abandoned the farm? That wasn't very responsible," Kione chimed in.

Son took a deep breath. He had traveled across the country by foot, learned how to read, fought a gang of hoodlums, and almost died. He wasn't going to be browbeaten by a couple of washed-up drunkards. He ignored his uncle's comment and addressed his father directly. "You left me there alone," he said sternly.

Agitated, his father shot back, "I knew you'd be fine. You have hair under your arms so you can take care of yourself!"

"You didn't even say anything," Son replied. "You just left. I thought you were dead!"

"That's your problem," the boozer answered uncaringly.

The boy's forehead wrinkled and his jaw tightened. "That's *my* problem?" he answered. "That's all you have to say?"

"What do you want from me?" his father yelled. "I told you that you were in charge!"

Son could feel his emotions escalate. A mixture of pain, rejection, and anger simmered inside of him. He wanted to speak out of the exasperation he felt, but instead, spoke what had been in his heart all along. "I don't want anything from you. I've only ever wanted you to be my father, and for you to treat me like your son."

"Hmmf," was all his father said with a put-out expression on his face. He lit a cigarette and took a deep drag, looking away from the boy.

"Why did you leave me to come here?" Son asked.

His father kept puffing at his cigarette without answering, but his uncle Kione seemed to be enjoying the argument. Perhaps he was weary of his brother-in-law's company, or maybe he just wanted to add salt to the boy's wounds. He spoke up, saying, "Before your mother lost her mind, she would squirrel money away into a nest egg for the two of you. It wasn't much but, as soon as word reached your father that she died, he rushed here to claim it, as well as her other belongings."

Son couldn't believe what he was hearing. All he could say was, "What?"

"He drank it all up," his uncle continued. "Now I can't get the idiot to leave."

Son's father made an obscene gesture towards Kione but said nothing.

"How could you do that?" Son asked his father heatedly.

His father said, "She owed it to me for having to take care of you!" in an angry, self-righteous tone.

Son stood there feeling like a dagger had been plunged into his chest. In his thoughts were both angry retorts and loving expressions aching to be spoken. He wanted to tell his father how much he loved him, and how much he'd been hurt by him. He wanted to tell him about his journey, about his friends, and about how much he'd grown. But he knew that his words would all be wasted. It dawned on him that whatever part of his father's mind that made him capable of being a caring parent was destroyed by liquor and hard living. He was simply incapable of loving him as a son. The realization broke the boy's heart and liberated him at the same time. It set him free to say good-bye.

Son's uncle smirked and said, "I think it's time for you to get back to the farm."

"I'm not going back to the farm," Son replied with confidence.

"I knew it!" his father responded. "You're selfish, just like your mother. You're a useless good-for-nothing!"

In the midst of the drunken, dysfunctional accusations,

Son took another deep breath. His posture was composed, but his eyes gave away a sadness. He said, "You're right. I wasn't good for much on the farm. But during my journey here, I discovered that I'm good at two things: enduring and walking. But I'm done enduring you, and now I'm walking away. Good-bye, Father."

As the boy turned to leave, his father chortled smugly and asked, "What's that supposed to mean?"

Son didn't bother to answer. He just walked out and closed the door behind him. In his heart, he had said good-bye forever. There was no need to explain himself, no use in making peace, and no point in even trying. He was free. It was a painful, sad freedom, but freedom nonetheless.

As Son walked away from his uncle's house, he was visibly upset. No one said a word as he and his companions moved down the street together. A myriad of scenarios played through the boy's mind as he walked. He imagined all the different ways the confrontation with his father could have gone. He imagined himself putting his father in his place with well-deserved criticisms. He imagined defending himself from the implications that he was selfish and useless. He even imagined breaking his uncle's nose with the hilt of his sword.

After a while, Dulnear broke the silence. He walked closely by Son's side, placed his hand on his shoulder, and asked, "Where are you going, Son?"

The boy looked at Dulnear with sad, tired eyes, and answered, "I don't know. I just want to be away from here," and he wiped a tear away from his cheek.

"I understand," the large man responded with empathy.

From behind, Maren asked, "Can we get something to eat?"

Son closed his eyes, shook his head, and suppressed a laugh. He was amused by the girl's inability to read the emotion of the situation, but also realized that remaining upset over things that he lacked the power to change would just needlessly torment him. "That's a great idea," he answered.

The three of them made their way to the east side of the city's center and returned to the pub they'd visited when they first arrived in Blackcloth. It was late in the afternoon, and the same rosy-cheeked barmaid who served them before brought their food out to them. Even though it wasn't that long ago since they'd dined there last, it felt to Son like it had been years.

Son was still hurting but felt comforted by the presence of his friends. They weren't perfect, but he trusted them. He understood them, and felt safe in their company. He knew they loved him and would, at least, treat him rationally. About midway through their meal, the boy suggested, "Let's go south."

Dulnear and Maren both looked at the boy with a slightly shocked expression. The man from the north asked, "Did you decide not to return to Aesef's farm?"

"Maybe someday," the boy answered. "But for now, I would like to get far away from Blackcloth."

Dulnear took a deep breath and asked, "All right, when do we leave?"

"I was thinking first thing in the morning," Son answered. "That is, if it's okay with the two of you."

Maren answered right away, "Okay."

Dulnear responded, "It will be nice to be back on the road again."

When the three of them had finished their early dinner, they checked into the inn that was situated above the pub. It was a small but clean room with two beds. Dulnear volunteered to sleep on the floor since he was too large for either of the beds anyway. He also slept better on hard surfaces.

There was still a small amount of light left in the sky when Dulnear and Maren fell asleep, but Son laid awake for a while. The combination of the pub's patrons talking noisily below and his racing thoughts kept him awake. He felt the heaviness of his mother's passing. Also, he replayed in his mind several times the encounter he'd had at his uncle's house. He hoped that he could fully forgive his father, and that the man would one day set his life on an honorable course. He was also nervous and excited about traveling south. Traveling to a place he'd never gone before was a bit uncomfortable, but the prospect of starting a new life, in a new place, made him feel like anything was possible.

Eventually, he fell asleep. As he slept, he dreamed of sleeping under open skies, the Southern Sea, and flying like the elder eagle.

CHAPTER FOURTEEN
A New Home

S ON WOKE EARLY THE NEXT morning. He was enthusiastic about putting his home city and the unhappy memories that were made there behind him. He had never been south before, but his mother had spoken of the southern coastlands when he was younger, and it sounded like a beautiful place.

They purchased the supplies they needed before they left Blackcloth, including a proper blanket for Son. He felt he had outgrown his horse blanket, but kept it around just in case. The trip south wouldn't be as long as the one from his father's farm and there were several villages along the way, so they weren't worried about running out of provisions while on the road.

Their journey only lasted a few weeks and, aside from stopping for a few days to earn money building stone fences, it was rather uneventful. None of them really minded though, after all they had experienced. Most nights they turned in early, and most mornings Son and Dulnear were up as soon as it was light enough to have a cup of coffee and read. It was a peculiar sight to see the large man from the north and the not-so-large boy, sitting in the same posture, sipping coffee, and reading books. Maren, however, had to be coaxed out of her slumber each day.

When they reached the southern coastland, Son felt like he was seeing the world for the first time. The road turned east and was at a higher elevation, running parallel with the coast. Every step offered a breathtaking view of the gently sloping forest and farmland meeting with the sea in the distance, and the boy did most of his walking with his head turned to the right, taking in the view. Even the gray skies couldn't detract from the joy of seeing the endless body of water from this vantage.

Eventually, they came upon the hamlet of Laor, a quaint and clean settlement with a pub, some shops, and a large inn. It was a short distance south of the easterly road, with a stunning view of the sea. As they walked into the community, Son noticed the friendly faces and the cheery disposition of the residents. It was much different from Blackcloth, and the boy felt very comfortable there.

The three walked to the pub and took a table outside, where they were able to share a meal and take in the view. As they did, Son asked, "Is there any reason we can't just stay here?"

Maren's eyes grew big and she smiled, answering, "I would like that very much!"

Dulnear also answered, "This would make a fine place to stay."

After some discussion about the details of settling into a new village, the man from the north went inside the pub to make inquiries about how he could go about finding land to rent in Laor. It was a somewhat refreshing experience for the man. Instead of the usual gawking and suspicious stares, he was greeted with lighthearted comments like, "Boy, you are a big one, aren't you?" and, "Remind me to stay on your good side!"

Dulnear introduced himself to the barkeep, who knew a patron, that had a cousin, who had a friend, that owned a textile shop in the village, who also had some land, with a house on it, for rent.

The property was about an hour's walk from Laor, but the owner took the travelers there by carriage, so it only took them a few minutes to arrive. There was enough land to grow a vegetable garden, and on it stood a barn, and a large old house that was badly in need of repair. The adjacent farms were sizable, and their houses and barns could not be seen easily, causing the rental property to feel much larger than it was. The owner offered to charge a smaller rent if the three were willing to make improvements to the old house, and they agreed. Son got the sense that the man had other financial interests, and didn't really see the farm as an important source of income. That detail was just fine for the boy, since he felt like he was renting a piece of paradise for a very fair price.

When everything was agreed to and the landlord rode off, Son could barely contain his excitement. The three of them surveyed the barn and house, and Dulnear made a list of materials and repair projects to do. There was much to be done, but they had a place of their own.

Days turned into weeks and eventually, the house became habitable as they repaired the roof and reinforced the floors. It was a two-story house, large enough for each of them to have a room of their own, with a sizable combined kitchen and living space on the first floor.

They also made repairs to the barn, and Son often used it as a workshop to make toys. Occasionally, the boy would take his creations to Laor and sell them to children in the square.

They also planted a vegetable garden. Son put Maren in charge of hoeing and pulling weeds. She seemed to enjoy the repetitive work and did it, most days, without reminding. She could often be heard talking and singing to herself as she labored.

Since they weren't traveling and camping every night, they could spend as much time as they wanted sharing stories, singing songs, and laughing into the dark hours. This new life very much agreed with them, but Son frequently felt homesick for the land of the Great Father. He didn't know when he would ever return there, and there just wasn't another experience in Son's whole imagination that could compare.

One day, as Son was making his way to the barn, Maren stopped him. The boy was a bit surprised and asked, "Are you okay?"

The girl said with a smile, "Come with me."

Son smiled and replied, "Where are we going?"

"You'll see," Maren answered, and she led him by the hand to the southern edge of the property, where Dulnear was waiting.

Surrounding the man from the north were several

large bouquets of beautiful flowers, held as high as he was, by branches fixed in the ground. Each branch had flowers running up and down itself as well. Some of them were joined by beautiful ribbon, and others stood alone. It was a delightful sight, and Son thoroughly enjoyed walking through what looked like an orchard of blossoms.

When the boy reached Dulnear, the man gave him a good-hearted smile, stepped to the side, and gestured to what was on the ground behind him. It was a vase of flowers, cast in iron, that stood to just above Son's waist. It was lovely and strong, and Son marveled at the craftsmanship that went into it; but he didn't see the most important part. Still unsure of what was happening, he asked, "Did you make this?"

"Yes," Dulnear answered. "Look closely at the vase."

When Son took a second look at the iron vase, he noticed a name impressed on the side of it, just below the lip. It read: "Brea."

When he read the name out loud, he got down on both knees and wept, for it was his mother's name. Dulnear joined him in kneeling around the memorial, as did Maren.

The man from the north put his arm around Son and said, "We wanted to honor your mother properly. We know that she meant so much to you."

"Thank you, Dulnear," the boy said through his weeping. "Thank you."

As they knelt there, Son shared his most cherished memories of his mother, and the three of them shared prayers and tears as they said good-bye to a woman who gave of herself selflessly to the son she loved. It was a meaningful moment for the boy that would remain fixed in his mind forever.

The months went on and the seasons changed. They eventually held a memorial for Maren's parents as well, right next to where they'd said good-bye to Son's mother. Dulnear made iron monuments for them, too, and for a long time, Maren would lay flowers by them every day.

It felt comforting to Son to be living in a way that had rhythm. He woke at the same time every morning, would spend his mornings working in the vegetable garden with Maren, his afternoons building toys in the shop, and his evenings relaxing with his friends. Occasionally, he would learn new fighting techniques and practice his swordsmanship, but mainly because the man from the north insisted on it.

Every few days, Son would walk to the village to sell his creations. He enjoyed earning the money, but he also made friends in the process. He met a few other boys his age, but most of his new acquaintances were grownups. He had a maturity and energy about him that they admired, and they were always impressed by the ingenuity and craftsmanship of the items he sold.

Dulnear spent most of his time restoring the house and barn. After all of the months they had been living there the house looked like new, as did the barn. It was a place they all felt proud to call home, and on the occasions when neighbors came calling, they were always full of compliments for what the three had done with the place.

One day, as Son was returning from the village, the

man from the north was waiting for him outside the house. "Good afternoon," the boy said cheerily.

"Hello, Son," Dulnear said with a sad smile.

Son immediately knew that something wasn't right. He asked, "What's going on?"

"Come sit with me," the man replied, and they walked over to some wooden chairs that were situated outside of the barn. Then he continued, as if wishing he did not have to, "Son, I have to take a journey."

"What do you mean? What kind of journey?" the boy asked.

"One that I have to take alone," Dulnear answered.

Son's heart sank when he heard those words. He remembered his emotions when he was alone on his father's farm, and a feeling of abandonment began to close in on him like a heavy fog. "How long will you be gone?" he asked.

"I don't know," the man from the north answered. "But I do plan to return, if I am able."

"If you're able?" the boy continued to inquire.

"Son, as you remember, I killed another man from the north when we fought near Blackcloth. It will only be a matter of time before Tromdel's family finds me here to take revenge," Dulnear explained. "I can't put you and Maren at risk by waiting for them to come here."

Feeling a sense of panic over losing his friend and mentor, the boy said, "But we can fight them. We'll be ready! You don't have to leave!" and tears began to fall down his cheeks.

"I know we can," the boy's faithful friend said as he placed his hand on his shoulder. "But, even if we defeated them, more would come. Revenge is the way of the north, and I don't want to subject you to an endless cycle of heartbreak and violence."

But Son's heart was already breaking. He asked, "So you're just going to run from this?"

"No, Son," Dulnear answered. "I'm running to it. The only way I can end this is if I go to Tromdel's family and offer myself to them in restitution."

"Restitution?!" Son repeated indignantly. "You were defending yourself! They should be apologizing to you!"

"I know, lad," the big man responded. "But violent men are irrational. They can be too blinded by anger to think clearly or act with wisdom."

"But they'll kill you!" Son continued to plead.

"Perhaps," Dulnear said. "Or maybe I'll be able to plead my case, and they will have mercy on me. Only the Great Father knows."

Son got out of his chair, wrapped his arms around his friend's neck, and squeezed as tightly as he could while he cried and cried.

Through his own tears, the man from the north said, "Oh, Son, you're such a strong lad. I know that you're going to be okay and that you're going to take great care of Maren. I'm going to miss you terribly, though," and the two of them cried great tears until they ran out.

When the boy regained his composure, he remained standing and asked, "When will you be leaving?"

"In a couple of weeks," the man answered. "I just want to make sure I didn't miss anything when mending the house and barn. I wouldn't want to leave you here and have you discover that there was more that needed repairing."

"Thank you," Son replied. "I'm not very handy with that sort of thing, but I hope to be someday."

Dulnear just looked at the boy proudly for a moment and said, "I love you, Son."

Son smiled in return and said, "I love you, too."

As Dulnear spent the next few days making the final repairs to the house, his heart was heavier than it had ever been. He mentally rehearsed many possible scenarios that didn't involve returning to the north, but he knew that they would all end with violence coming to their home near Laor.

The man felt nervous about leaving the children, even though Son was more than ready to handle another man like the one from the tavern. As a precaution, he reinforced the house door to withstand any aggressor, and he engineered iron shutters that could be slid over the windows from the inside. He also installed a door to gain access to the roof and a way to escape the house from under the kitchen floor. In addition, he left bows and arrows, an extra sword, and a dagger in various locations around the house. It may have been overkill, but he was from the north, and readiness was his nature.

As his time with his fellow travelers drew to a close, he found himself praying often for the strength to do what must be done. He had slain fierce warriors, led many battles, and remained undefeated in combat, but this was the most difficult thing he had ever done.

The next two weeks went by much faster than Son hoped they would. He had the unhappy task of explaining to Maren that their dear friend would be leaving. She didn't seem very sad at the moment, but was even more withdrawn and quiet than usual for the next few days. The conversation around the farm was light, and a little dry, because no one was sure what to talk about with the sadness of Dulnear's departure looming over them.

When the day finally came for Dulnear to leave, Son made a hearty breakfast for everyone; partly as an act of kindness, and partly to make their final moments together last a little longer. He secretly longed to beg the man to stay but put on a brave, supportive face. He hoped with all that was in him that he would see his friend again one day.

When they were finished eating and talking, the man from the north prepared to leave by belting on his weapons and donning his long fur coat. The sight of the man ready for the road stirred up powerful memories and emotions in Son, and he fought back tears that were aching to come out.

When he was ready to leave, Dulnear reached inside of his bag and produced the three bags of gold they had recovered from the man from the tavern. "I almost forgot," he said as he placed the gold on the kitchen table. "These belong to Maren. Use them to take care of her. When she is able to care for herself, what remains will be hers to do with as she pleases. Let no one know about it."

"I understand," the boy answered.

The three of them exited the house and walked up to the road together. It was cool and windy, and they walked slowly, but didn't say anything. Finally, Son broke the silence and said, "Safe travels to the north."

"Thank you, lad," Dulnear replied. He looked sad, but was also holding himself together, for the boy's sake. He bent down and said good-bye to Maren with a hug and a kiss on the cheek, saying, "I'll miss you, little friend."

Maren hugged him back and said, "I'll miss you," as a tear ran down her face.

Then Son hugged Dulnear one last time. It was the tightest squeeze he had ever given anyone, for he never wanted to let go, and the man from the north did in kind. As they ended their embrace, the boy noticed something strange and puffy protruding from the man's coat. "What is that?" he asked as he pointed at the object.

"It's an elder eagle," his friend said as he pulled the stuffed toy bird from his coat. "Maren made it for me." He gave the girl a wink, and she smiled proudly in return. He then carefully put the gift back in his coat before the wind had a chance to carry it away.

Not wanting the moment to end, Son and Dulnear just looked at each other. Then the boy spoke sincerely, "Thank you for all you've done for me."

"You're a man now, Son, and a warrior at that," his friend encouraged. "Just don't ever forget what matters most."

Son remembered all of the things Dulnear had taught him during their time together, and he remembered the words that the Great Father spoke to him. Before he had a chance to respond to Dulnear's final counsel, a gust of wind parted the clouds over the farm. It surprised the boy, and he marveled at the color of the sky and the golden hue that was cast over everything. "Look, the sky is blue!" he exclaimed.

"The sky has always been blue," Dulnear responded. "You just couldn't see it past the clouds." He then paused and smiled at the boy, and said, "Good-bye, my friend."

"Good-bye," Son said in return, and he watched the warrior begin his journey to Tuas-Arum.

Son and Maren stood there and continued watching the man from the north walk down the road. As they did, Son prayed that he would see his friend again one day. He knew that his life, and his home, would feel empty without him, and he was thankful for the time they'd had together.

When Dulnear was no longer in sight, Maren asked Son, "Would you tell me that story about the stars again?"

The boy smiled and looked at her caringly, saying, "Gladly."

They then made their way to the chairs that were outside the barn, where they spent the rest of the morning sharing stories and memories of their adventures. When they were done, Son sat alone for a while, pondering the last chapter of his life, and dreaming of a bright future.

CHAPTER FIFTEEN
EPILOGUE

I T WAS YEARS LATER, AND Son was now a man. He was still smaller than average, but he was a giant on the inside. Maren was also grown. She loved the farm near Laor so much that she purchased it from the landlord when Son left her in charge of her family inheritance.

Son decided that it would be a good thing to take some time to travel alone. He still had a fondness for walking, and was halfway through a season of exploring the roads of Aun by foot. It was a time of reflection, and it was refreshing for him. Even though he could afford to stay at inns each night, he often chose to camp.

One late afternoon, he was enjoying a meal in a busy pub. It was loud and rowdy, but he remained focused on a book he was reading as he ate and sipped stout from a large mug. He had just closed his book and taken the last bite of his meal when he noticed an awkward-looking boy enter the bar. The boy wore ill-fitting clothing and looked overwhelmed by the unruly atmosphere of the place.

Son watched as the youngster approached the counter and asked the barkeep a question. The irritable barkeep shook his head and waved the boy away. As the lad approached the door to leave, two drunken ne'er-do-wells stopped the boy and began harassing him. It was a scene that provoked Son's sense of justice and compassion, and he watched carefully as he drank the remainder of his beer.

After the boy managed to get past the men and out the door, Son continued to keep an eye on the drunkards as they laughed and congratulated each other for their ability to bully a helpless child. Predictably, one of them suggested that they go after the boy to harass him some more. A few seconds after they exited the bar, Son calmly stood up from his table, placed his book inside of his bag, grabbed the large metal beer stein he had been drinking from, and followed them.

I hope you enjoyed reading "Son of the Age". It is a project that is very near and dear to me. If you would like information about my next book, "Man from the North" as well as other forthcoming projects, please visit my website at www.leebezotte.com and sign up for my e-newsletter.

Thank you for journeying with me!
Lee Bezotte

Made in the USA
Columbia, SC
04 May 2020

95754871R10117